PORNY STORIES
SHORT STORIES

EVA MORAN

PORNY STORIES
SHORT STORIES

Cover illustration by Katrinn Pelletier, colagene.com.
Author photograph by John Paul Cragg.
Book designed and typeset by Primeau & Barey, Montreal.
Edited by David McGimpsey for the Punchy Writers Series.

Copyright © Eva Moran, 2008.
Legal Deposit, *Bibliothèque et Archives nationales du Québec*
and the National Library of Canada, 4th trimester, 2008.

Library and Archives Canada Cataloguing in Publication
Moran, Eva, 1975-
Porny stories/Eva Moran.
ISBN 978-1-897190-45-6 (bound).
ISBN 978-1-897190-44-9 (pbk.)
1. Title.
PS8626.O733P67 2008   C813'.6   C2008-906423-2

This is a work of fiction. Names, characters, places, and events are either products of the author's imagination or are employed fictitiously. Any resemblance to actual events or locales or persons, living or dead, is entirely coincidental.

No part of this publication may be reproduced or stored in a retrieval system or transmitted in any form or by any means, electronic, mechanical, recording, or otherwise, without written permission of the publisher, DC Books.

In the case of photocopying or other reprographic copying, a license must be obtained from Access Copyright, Canadian Copyright Licensing Agency,
1 Yonge Street, Suite 800, Toronto, Ontario M5E 1E5 <info@accesscopyright.ca>

For our publishing activities, DC Books gratefully acknowledges the financial support of the Canada Council for the Arts, of SODEC, and of the Government of Canada through the Book Publishing Industry Development Program (BPIDP).

     Canada Council   Conseil des Arts
                         for the Arts   du Canada

*Société
de développement
des entreprises
culturelles*
Québec ❖❖

Printed and bound in Canada by Marquis Imprimeur. Interior pages printed on 100 per cent recycled and FSC certified Silva Enviro white paper.
Distributed by Lit DistCo.

DC Books
PO Box 666, Station Saint-Laurent
Montreal, Quebec H4L 4V9
www.dcbooks.ca

For my father

CONTENTS

- 9   How I Want You
- 31   Quiz: Is a Genius Loving You
- 35   Old
- 57   How to Date a Mezzo
- 61   How Could You Hate Your Mother? (Let Me Tell You)
- 73   How to Date a Writer
- 83   *Julius Caesar:* a Play Review
- 87   Bun Head
- 97   Centerfold
- 107   *I Am America (And So Can You!):* a Book Review
- 111   The Glad Garbage-bag Man: a Psychological Portrait in Film
- 117   Are You Dating a Man Ready for Middle-class Marriage?
- 123   Tell Me. Why Does He Have to Have a Head?
- 135   How an Internet Quiz Saved My Love-life and Made Me Some Money too
- 139   This Story is Wearing a Labcoat: Very Scientific!
- 151   How to Date a Gay Man
- 155   Dylan Begee Hated My Vibrator
- 169   Jared: a Psychological Portrait of a Subway Dauphin in CD's
- 173   How to Date a Lawn Bowler
- 177   Chuck-Chik
- 185   I Tend to the Tail End

HOW I WANT YOU

I want you to want me.

I visited this friend of mine, Mayler, down in Florida. Mayler and me, we are just friends. But not really really. He wants me. And I used to want him.

You are nothing like Mayler.

Just before I got on the plane to come home, Mayler told me that I suffer from low self-esteem. When I asked him why, he told me it was because my golf swing was too stiff. That, plus I'd fucked too many guys.

"Anyone that fucks that many guys has to have low self-esteem."

I told him to massage his balls with a Tabasco sauce rubbing alcohol cut-glass cocktail. But not really. Really I said, "I can play a pretty good game of golf man!" and then rushed to the car to sulk.

When he gets into the driver's side I imagine that there is a wall all around me. He can't get to me.

Low self-esteem, my ass!

But now this is all I think of. I think of my low self-esteem.

In a panic, I turn to my most trusted source: *Cosmo*. Some people may think that the How To's and Quizzes in chick-mags are only as useful as statistics about cars that have gone over a cliff while driving with a platypus in the passenger seat, but I swear by them. Since grade seven when I was desperately trying to understand why the boys didn't like-like me and the quiz *Which Fairytale Princess Are You?* let me know that I was Snow White the tom-boy princess with many male friends but only one true prince, to today when *Why Don't Men Approach You?* explains that I am too confident and not insecure at all, I have trusted all chick-lit sources. They are an indispensable resource. The most important thing: they make me right, and Mayler wrong.

Thank you *Cosmo*, I feel strong again.

Until breakfast.

I ordered my Huevos Rancheros and we, the ladies, were talking about dating. And I said, "I don't think it's too much to ask that he doesn't have a girlfriend. I mean, ditch her. I'm great..." about some guy on a balcony who told me he loves me–a story I just made up. And then as a joke, because of course I told all my friends what Mayler said, "Op! There I go again with my low self-esteem." And everyone laughed. And I should've felt great, right? but I didn't. I thought, "Am I even good?"

It's like by saying the words, insecure, low-self-esteem, lack of confidence, Mayler conjured them into existence. Mayler's like a witch that way, or a druid or a wizard. Or whatever a dude-witch is called–that's Mayler: conjurer of insecure. I'm not even sure I'll ever be able to play a game of golf again. And I can't fuck anyone—anyone outside of my daydreams.

I dream about you—the you I want to want me, which could be everyone or anyone at any given time but today it's you. I should say, these days it's you.

I've thought about it every way and everywhere. I've thought about it in a bed. I've thought about it on a boat. I've thought about it in a castle with a moat. I've thought about it up high and down low. I've even thought about it starting with a peep-show.

Okay. Fine. I'm using the Seuss as a distancing mechanism. But, still, I swear, it's all deeply true even if I need a system.

Greg used to tell me that—that I had a Pentagon defense system: the Pentagon gone Mother Goose.

He said, "No one's ever getting close to you."

But that's not true. He could have got close to me but he wouldn't tear my clothes off. He liked us both to undress neatly first and then climb into bed having folded our respective garments. He came in the room once and I was lying there waiting and he asked, "Why don't you get undressed?" And still I waited, watching him slide his khacki pants to his ankles. "Oh. You expect me to tear your clothes off." He snorted like it was a funny idea.

It was a long staring competition. Him naked. Standing. Me clothed. Waiting. It was winter. How long could he wait? I asked myself how long I could wait when he began to double-fist his cock and pump it hard.

But I know what I want.

I put my folded clothes to the side of the bed.

My favorite way to think of you these days is like we're in a romance novel or something. Like I dream of you there... at the bike shop. All sweaty and hard from being a sweaty hard bike mechanic. And, there's me. It's a blowzy spring day. I'm wearing a red summer dress very à la mode, very revealing and I walk into your shop through the automatic doors and the fragrant air breezes in with me and you see me and you wrap your grease stained hands around me and slide them down my ass and grip so firm and deep that I can feel your fingers push into me and get wet.

Or, we are on the beach at night sitting on some driftwood. My red dress is billowing in the wind. I'm cold. You ask, "Are you cold?" And I straddle you and get inside your jacket and smell you and you have a good smell—the kind of smell I can smell for life. And I grab for your belt buckle and it's cold but I'm not. I'm hot. I whisper, "God you make me hot." And I fuck you backwards watching the ocean, I come and I tell you you made me come. And then you make me beg for it. I whisper, "Please. Please. Please." And then you bend me over the driftwood and fuck me deep and hard and harder and then hardest, deep. And then you cum all over my back. And I love it.

Or or or, there is this one. I am standing at the kitchen counter in a red dress and I ask you to put your hands on me and....

I really need to buy a red dress.

The reality. I went to see you last summer. After coffee you asked me what else I wanted to do. There you were, gorgeous and manly–bicep manly–standing there like a man–manly. Waiting. I could have said anything. It was summer. And I was wearing a summer dress. And I did want to go down to the beach to go down on you. I looked in the direction of the water and then at you.

"I dunno. This city's kinda dead at night," I said.

And you said, "People are so weird. And totally predictable. It's boring, right? But magnolia trees and cherry trees in blossom captivate us every goddamn spring… it's just doing what it does… forever and always. Bastard trees! Know what I mean?"

"Yeah."

What did you mean? Are you actually a bike mechanic? Are you like a flower philosopher gay bike mechanic?

"Did I tell you you look good tonight? You do. Nice dress. Keep in touch."

You hold me for a little too long.

I will keep in touch. God! I will. I'll touch myself while we keep in touch. I'll cross my heart and swear to you: I will think of you and touch myself.

I haven't wanted anyone as badly as I've wanted you.

I thought that only dirty old men like Dante got to have little girl muses inspiring them to wax poetic straight into the classical cannon but now I know that all you have to be is dirty and then you're set; you are my muse.

It started out as poetry in my journals. Long epic poems about flowers and you fucking me. But I am a shitty poet. And the poems just turned into a stream of musings about you my muse until I had oodles of lusty lines making hot stories that made me and my friends hot. So I thought why not send the stories out? Why not go for what Dante went for—poetic fame, grandeur, and perfection?

That's how I ended up at Harlequin.

With you as my muse and the Harlequin formula this whole new love world was so easy. There's a guy. There's a needy girl. There's veiled sex. There's a fight. There's a rescue. And then, there's love—real romantic love.

It was so so easy at first. I just plugged you and me in.

For example, my first book: I have two kids alone because my husband died in a tragic DUI on our anniversary. To make ends meet and buy my little girls a bicycle, I become an elf. You are Santa Claus. Together, we are perfect mall mythology.

Late one night we're snowed-in at the mall. Just me and you.

Oh dear! How do I get to my daughters? Are they safe? What should we do Santa? What should we do?

You lean over me and say, "We're not real. We can do whatever we want. We can make magic."

Did we ever!

I called it *Yes I Can Can for Santa*. Masterpiece! I think.

But then, my Fabio gets the pink slip.

When I walk into the boardroom on the third floor of Flagship-romance I'm sweating through two shirts. I walk into a wall of lady-angular editors.

Okay. So. Umm. Maybe Santa bounce-bounce bouncing me on his knee while I tell him what I want was a bit much but, but, but.... I cut the part where we get high and employ the manikins in a hard elf labor camp of our love. Maybe the bad idea was the climax saloon scene when after you watched flashes of my pussy as I kicked high into the air, you buy my daughters two pink bikes that we christen in our love juices. Uhh... yeah. Maybe that was a little much.

"We at Harlequin," starts Mab the head-bitch in black, "don't know what you were thinking?"

Stupid stupid stupid! Sex should always be wearing an alluring transparent nightie! Our sex was a topless Jarvis street crack-head hooker.

"Neither do I. Sorry."

God. What was I thinking? That I could write?

Mab's assault continues, "There was no marriage. No real rescue outside of some vague reference to euphoric orgasm interpreted as love. And where was the fight?"

"Oh. I just tucked it in there between, ummm, the uhhh, first love and second love... scenes."

"Well. It's all wrong for Harlequin."

"I know I'm sorry. Sorry. I'll just ahh...."

Everyone shuffles in their seats. Some start to collect their papers.

"I really appreciate the opportunity you...."

Can they take their money back? Fuckety-fuck-pants! My new lap-top. I'll have to take my new lap-top back.

"But we love it for our new imprint."

Everything in the room stops.

"In this urban fem, post-fem world full of eye-candy and boy toys, chick-lit and the New York bitch chic of I know what I want and you are not it but you can be it for now until the morning... we like the idea of more boys, less feeling."

"Well, yeah but, like you said there was some sort of love even if misinterpreted and there was only one guy."

"Huh."

Mab peers over her MaxMara black-rimmed glasses and brushes my sentence away with a flick of her hand.

"More men. Less feeling. The main character can struggle with some feelings, maybe even end up in some tentative traditional romance B.S., but we'd prefer just play, games and lots of sex and maybe a fight somewhere. Think Madonna, Christina Aguilera, Pam Anderson. Think fuckaliscious, fuckglorious, fuck-happy."

More like a drive-through McFuckrappy meal. I think.

She's so angular.

"I only write about one guy, really."

Mab is looking at me hard. Sizing me up without looking me up and down. She's just taking me all in. The other ladies are just sitting there, nonchalant, listening, not caring, waiting for pointy Mab to give the go-ahead to jump on my throat. Or, worse, forget about me.

"Look. Can you do it or not?"

There is no way.

"Sure I can."

She smiles. They all do. And I feel ivory white and doe-eyed and poisoned by an old lady's creepy apple.

"Good. Rough draft by the end of the month."

The papers begin to ruffle and briefcase clasps go snap–the lady editors are all in a chatter.

And then, silence.

Mab speaks, "I want to read it personally."

I can feel it. This is going to be shitty.

I have to go home and tuck all my Harlequins away. This breaks my heart. I love the pictures on the covers. Those are real people on the covers. Real women posing in real bodices with real men really undoing them. How can you even undo a bodice by yourself? YOU CAN'T. How would I have gotten my daughters bikes without you? What am I going to do without my Fabio, you? What?

I try to write. But I can't.

You are nowhere. Without you, I am lost. There is no shore. I have no idea which way to go. With no idea how to get to you, I am adrift in a blank white sea. But I know I have to swim. Swim or Mab will sink me.

I backstroke. On high school swim team backstroke was my best. I can manage a fair clip and I do. I'm going and going and going and I have no real idea where I am headed but who cares, at least I'm going. And things start to change so I must be going somewhere. The water is salty. And this is pretty cool to be in a white sea swimming–swimming as fast as I can. And there are other people. 1940s movie star sailors all in white–like Gene Kelly and Sinatra. Wow! I've always really liked Gene Kelly and Sinatra. Sweet. And we're all swimming along in the White Sea and as we go the water gets denser and I move slower but I'm okay, I'm still givin' 'er and the sailors are still smiling their pearly white smiles. And so what if things are getting a bit… sticky? Smiling sailors, Cetaphil-texture, salty, sticky… water? Oh god. Seamen semen! I'm stroking sailor spunk. Thousands of sailors and gallons of spunk. This grosses me out.

I yell out, "This fucking grosses me out man!"

But the sailors just keep on smiling. The waves of cum lapping my body. The endless deep thrumming of thousands of fists pumping.

This is all too much for me. I'm weak. I can't do this. I can't take this sailor gang-bang. I'm just not woman enough.

And I let go. I let go and lapse and fall and sink.

Down.

Down.

Down.

Into the deep deep dark.

And here at the bottom, I can hear–I can hear myself better than I ever have. And I want to stay. I want to stay in this solitary silence away from it all forever.

But I can't.

She whispers, "You can't."

And I feel her strong hand on my back.

Mermaid Marion.

She carries me swift to shore and drops me off.

Mermaid Marion puts all the sailors in a row. Puts them all in a row to knock them down to their knees.

And I say, "That's cool. What else can you do besides saving lives and making men worship you?"

And Mermaid Marion says, "I can do lots of cool stuff on land. On land I have lots of special powers."

Mostly her special powers are fucking men.

"You can be like my invisible side-kick," she says to me. "You can just write down whatever I do."

Mermaid Marion puts on her red dress and takes the town. She has a new date every night. And every night she gets laid. And sometimes she makes disturbing analogies that I love to copy down, like "Really I'm just a barnyard milkmaid: I yank until they cream-scream." I love this one. It's demeaning and it disturbs me. I love it. And sometimes when she's fucking and I'm watching on the sidelines she moos and yells, "I do it to amooooos you!" and the guy thinks it's about him when really it's for little invisible me.

And Mermaid Marion never loses her cool.

Okay, except for maybe once. But she was in the right. I mean, she hit on this guy at the bar.

She said, "Can I suck your cock? I'd like to suck your cock a lot."

And this guy says, "You shouldn't ask. You shouldn't have to ask. You should make me beg for it. Any woman worth screwing knows how...."

And Mermaid Marion's raven hair starts to wave around uncontrollably and her tawny skin is turning blush red and her eyes are fixed on him and I have no idea what is going to happen.

His mouth just keeps on talking and he asks, "Don't you have any self-respect?" and that is the last thing he ever says because Mermaid Marion blasts him with fire rays from her eyes and hair and he disintegrates right before us.

When I look at the knoll of corpse-ash at my feet I say the only thing I can, "That is so cool. When I was nine, I wanted to be a fire-starter. Whoa!"

And we just go on after that. Her fucking. Me writing her fucking. And she says she's like this because of a broken heart but that now her career is more important to her.

"I'm a rock-star/lawyer/psychologist/mother. It's very demanding and fulfilling."

Wow, I think. That's some pretty important job M.M.

And everything is la-di-da wonderful until one day she gets a call on her shell phone.

"Uh-huh. Okay. I see. Uh-huh. Well okay. Let me talk to her about it first. Yeah. Yeah. Okay. I will. See you soon."

My heart is broken.

"But you have to try to understand," she pleads. "There is a very important concert/case that I think would be very good for my patients and children if I play/win it. I have to go back to Kingdom Bumbpasea-c. I just have to."

I understand.

"I'll miss you," I say as I hand her her red dress and lip gloss.

"You keep those," she says. "I won't need them where I'm going."

And she stands there topless.

"M.M., you can't go out in the city like that!"

"Why not? These are all I need."

And she straps two rounded cushions to either shoulder: tackle ready.

I say, "Yeah. We used to have something like that in the eighties."

"Bye," she says.

I say, "Bye."

And that's that. All that's left of her is a red dress, lip-gloss and a manuscript. I line them up side by side on my bed. I write on the blank page of the book: *Milk Run in a Red Dress*. And I think, "Mab, is going to fry me."

This is how the meeting goes down:

"It's like *Battlestar Galactica*, Madonna, *The Little Mermaid*, Vonnegut, Freud and Jung all had a gorgy post-post fem queer modern culture fuck! Orgy! It's a.... Gorgysporg!"

Who's-a-what's-a-who's-it?

"I love it. Love it! It will sell. Oh my god will it sell. I like it so much I want to change the name of the imprint to Red Dress. Of course the title will just be *Milk Run*. WHAT. DO. YOU. THINK?"

Mab is all softscreen Mab and smiling—not pointy or sharp at all—it's like she's friendly, almost.

I don't know what to think.

When I go home, all the evidence minus the manuscript is still there on the bed. I think back to school. Back to my time as an undergrad at York when I took a delinquent psych class. I caught Jung in Mab's rant. I think Jung. I think: two personalities, two chemical substances; if there is any reaction, both are transformed, forever. I think me+you=x. And the x looms. Question.

I have no idea what you and me equal. I have never tried.

I look down at the limp red dress.

I decide to write to you as M.M. would.

>   Subject: I want you to do such wrong things to my body.
>
>   Hi,
>
>   I want you to do the dirtiest....
>
>   No. No. Wait.
>
>   I want you to take me like a....
>
>   No. Wait.
>
>   I want....
>
>   I want....

....

I want you to punish my pussy–my entire body–relentlessly with your cock.

....

and then maybe we can do coffee.

I hit Send.

You respond. Five seconds later.

Re: I want you to do such wrong things to my body.

I'm in town. Meet me at the Jetfuel. Tomorrow 7:30 p.m.?

Yes! Yes! Yes! I get to wear the red dress. I get to wear the red dress for you.

The next day, I am still in my happy world of success–book success and potential sex success–I hear a "blewp" from my computer and I race to it thinking it is you and I am elated–ELATED. And it's Mayler and not you. But I don't care. I want to brag.

So I g-chat with him about the book and how I thought I almost lost the same job twice and about how wicked-awesome you are and how I am going to see you tomorrow night and I tell him what I am going to wear and....

He writes, "Sorry."

I don't feel so good.

"I wrote to say I am sorry for saying those things about you."

I write, "Sorry that you said them?"

"If I had known that they would hurt you, I would never have said them."

"But you still think I have low self-esteem right?"

"I don't think it's really going to do either of us any good to talk about this any further."

"You brought it up."

I wait.

Nothing.

"I've done all sorts of good, crazy-good things. Why do you think it? Why?"

Nothing.

"Mayler, you are not some oracle with a riddle. I just want the answer. Why?"

Nothingnothingnothing. Never.

"WELL I'M NOT WAITING, MAYLER!"

I'm. Not. Waiting. This time.

I am not waiting for anything or anyone. I close my lap-top. And I chant. I won't wait. I won't wait. I won't wait like I did.

Like I did when I wanted it bad and went over to Jason's house wearing heels, thigh highs, a black and silver teddy, and a lot of make-up. I kissed him long. He changed me into oversized duck pj's—and watched 'til I fell asleep. Then he fucked me. Or Chris. Chris would spoon me and then "wake" from his deep "sleep" to feel me up. If I reacted he would drop back to "sleep." Only if I lay there still would he give me the full score and addendum. Then there was Sid and Ming. Both had an obsession with *Star Wars* sex. Actually it was worse: it was *Star Wars* prequel sex. I'd spend hours watching droid battles until comatose and then I'd get lazy sex: fucked while reclining on my side, on a couch, TV in plain view. Sid or Ming did not want to miss a moment—not one single *Star Wars* plasma screen moment. For all of them I would sit there in agony pretending to study or pretending to sleep or pretending to enjoy Jar Jar's witty repartee. Wanting. Staring. Monitoring my breathing. Only when I was a good possum, a nearly dead possum, a Sleeping Beauty neurotic desperate possum would I receive rescue—a touch—a call to filthy glossy cheap un-airbrushed wild.

Fuck *Star Wars*!

And fuck waiting.

Wanting badly and waiting sadly is over.

I'm not waiting for anything or anyone. Not for Mayler and not even for you.

"I swear, I won't wait for you," I say to myself.

"And I am not dolling up for you either."

Screw the red dress.

I throw on my black cons and my black jeans and a grey T and head out the door just as is: ready to see you.

And, when we meet, I just complain. You say let's go for a walk when the Jetfuel closes and we walk. And, I tell you about the whole thing. Mayler, golf, the books, Kingdom Bumbpasea-c. And maybe you think I'm totally crazy-girl crazy but I don't care. Walking. Walking. And more. About how my daddy beat me and my cat Tom died when I was seventeen and I had to leave class because I was crying so hard. And about each and every boyfriend. And I tell you everything but it's still not everything and then, you touch my collar bone.

"You're surprising."

And just like an emergency button for a loopty-loop I stop, dead. And you touch me. And breathe.

You say, "I bet you have a pretty mean golf swing." And you move your hand across my chest like you are flattening out a cool sheet of music and I feel myself open.

I look into your eyes—your sea-green eyes. You open me. Like a flower in spring. Like the one thousand million love stories and poems I am alluding to: You, open, me.

You say, "I see you."

All the light of childhood summers in a field or at the beach or in the park pours in. I feel hot and happy like those kids who really need some Kool-aid on a humid day and that big jug guy comes over and pours his orange icy-ness all over them. You are pouring over me with your hands.

"You're like my Kool-aid on a sticky summer's day," I say.

What the fuck did I just say?

You just stare at me.

Oh God! What the fuck did I just say? I'm about to cry.

"I know," you breathe. "I want you too."

And you start to undo my pants. And I can see me in your eyes and if I look hard enough I can see you in mine and me in yours again and again and again right into the future. Right into you drawing me a bath in winter after a hard afternoon. And I trust you haven't bent anyone else over and fucked them that day or on any other day, ever. And when you ask if I want Thai, you can reach into my purse without flinching because you know I am not your mother; I won't hurt you. My purse is your purse. With me, you can put your hands everywhere.

I want you from now, to then, to then, to then until we are old. I want you when your ears have grown to half the size of your head and your mouth and nose have grown together. I want to grow older closer together like your old nose and your old mouth on your future old face.

You whisper in my ear as you touch me, "God I want you."

And for a split second I think, what's wrong with you?

You ask, "No?" but I say, "Yes."

And this, all this, is exactly how I want you.

QUIZ: IS A GENIUS LOVING YOU

(This is how an internet quiz saved my relationship.)

Testimonial: When I walked into the washroom to find my husband looking at darling-faced Japanime girls in impossibly short skirts while he tickled his balls, I was incensed. But now, after taking "Is a Genius Loving You," I realize he was just being highly intellectual. I have something special with someone special. There's nothing quite like being loved by a genius.

Answer Yes or No to these 10 easy questions and discover if you have a special kind of love.

1. Is your boyfriend/husband named after an obscure Norwegian folkloric character?

2. Do you find yourself at home together, yet you are still ignored?

3. Is it hard for you to understand what your boyfriend's/husband's friends say to you when they are speaking in your language?

4. Do you miss having a boyfriend/husband who is a beer guy? Who likes... sports, other than fencing?

5. If you have any children, adopted or otherwise, does he seem to have a "close" relationship with any or all of them?

6. Is his hobby child-portrait photography?

7. Can your boyfriend's/husband's name be pornographied: For example, Ludwig Wittgenstein transforms into Ooooo! I would lud to wig wit his geshtein or, more simply, Albert Einstein in the cruel but fun rhyme, little Albert Einey likes to take it in the heiney?

   (Note: Some geniuses are not for fun, especially the utilitarianists. See below.)

John Stuart Mill

not for fun

8. Do you find your boyfriend/husband completely socially inept? Saying inappropriate things at parties or functions to strangers such as, "I write music as a sow pisses," or, "It's this disease I have; I just have to sex a lot of women... what are you doing later?"

9. Does he have any quirky behavior? Does he call his friends and ramble, ramble into the night? Does he pick at his face, draw incessantly or collect and catalogue his own stool?

10. Finally, do you do all the work and get none of the credit?

If you answered yes to 6 or more of these questions, CONGRATULATIONS to you dear lady, a genius is loving you!

(Huh. And here I thought Gints[1] was just an asshole. I guess I won't dump him.)

---

1. It may be out of your hands by now but I noticed one more mistake on page 57. Stripped should be striped. It may be out of your hands by now but I noticed one more mistake on page 57. Stripped should be striped. Gints Bygaimeister after Peer Gynt (look it up under Ibsen, you dumb bitch).*

* Footnote provided by Mr. Bygaimeister.

OLD

I am an average woman over 30. I have double bum—the regular bum and the cellulite bum just underneath regular bum. And, in the breast department, I am lacking in perk. Generally, over 30, my life is lacking in perks. I am no longer a hot item on the date list, the getting noticed on the street list, or the getting laid list.

So I go on dates with my friends.

Today, I'm going to the movies with Daniella.

I picked a Helena Bonham Carter pic because she's older than me; it won't damage my ego to see her naked on screen. And it doesn't. She sags all over.

I am not the pretty girl, woman, whatever, but my dates are.

Daniella Stats: Daniella does not sag or have double bum. You remember that Violent Femme song that went, "36-24-36! I want lots of pretty chicks!" Daniella. Yep. So what she's got a rockin' bod? Whatever, right? She's also that French chick with the poreless skin and thick wavy dark hair and, and here's the kicker, blue eyes. OH! Blue eyes and dark hair. It's like raw power packed into a little lady.

And when Daniella unleashes it, does she ever.

Daniella is a man crusher. Not an eater. Not like in my drunk twenties when scrawny me would go to the campus pub and get wasted on jello-shooters night after night going through new boys like most people use toilet paper. No. Daniella–Daniella's like a woman–like a soul destroying man crusher.

"I hate the cock. Yes? Its pokey little head. Poke. Poke. Poke. And its veins. It recalls to me my grandmother's hand when she would pet her parakeet. The blue, very blue veins and the stroking of the bird. Uhhh! Disgusting cock."

I don't tell her. If she hates the thing she comes by so easily, maybe I'm on the wrong course with cock. See. I love cock. I want cock. But I never get any cock. I really want cock.

But if Daniella doesn't, I will pretend I don't, and maybe that's just what will bring cock to me. She hates it and it just falls right in her lap.

Once, we were on this subway and there was this hot guy staring at Daniella so intense, aggressive–so straight–like a punch in the mouth.

She just stares back. Right back.

"Will you pass to me your mobile?" her hand out.

I riffle through my bag desperate to give her what she wants.

I have no idea what's going to happen. But I'm excited.

She holds out my phone pointing it at him like she's taking aim–a gun targeted between his eyes. And as she is typing she turns to me and says, "This is for you."

"Number." She blurts at hottie.

"W-w-what?" he says.

"Oh fuck," she says. "Fuck. You are like this cartoon pig."

"Porky Pig," I whisper.

She is awesome.

"Yes. This Porky the Pig. I can't date a pig."

"Date?"

His face is so confused. He's insulted, insulted yet excited all at once.

Daniella's really keeping him on his toes.

"Oh my God! And so quick too. What a catch." She flips the phone shut and is making to hand it back.

"No! No. I. Do. Not. Stammer. And, I. Really want. To give you. My number."

"Good. Good boy. Okay. Shoot."

She types away, hands me my phone and turns her back on the guy.

He gets off the train. He stares into our car and stammers, "Tim. My name is Tim. Uh. Nice to meet you."

Daniella looks back over her shoulder and grunts, "Uh-huh."

The doors close.

Poor little Timmy.

For a second I feel sorry, sorry and sympathetic and all empathetic for his poor dejected self but then all those human sharing emotions are replaced, taken over. By....

Moxy. So sexy: moxy. Man crusher. So cool.

Daniella.

I wish I could crush a guy.

No.

Wait.

I wish a guy had a crush on me. Helplessly. The way everyone does on Daniella, even including me. Addicted. We're a world of crazed diabetics let into a sugar-free sweet shop where Daniella's the only treat. She has complete control.

It may sound crazy but it's true!

When Daniella gets off the train all eyes are on her. The train pulls away and sweeps her hair back and up. She jaunts along the platform smiling like a mad conqueror–like Stalin or Hitler might have in their prime photo-ops if they hadn't been so serious–like if they had been wind-blown 1980s friendly super models–Stalin or Hitler as Cindy Crawford.

Daniella is beautiful. Like a Czar supermodel megalomaniac.

She exudes all of those womanly things that strong women are supposed to be.

You know?

Good woman stuff.

Sexuality, smarts, independence, a loving nature, softness, a peppering of hardness, a joie de vivre, commitment, excitement, an ability to be alone, style, sensuous lips, a great laugh, a pinch of tears with good timing, an effortless hairdo, a short time in the bathroom, a liking of scotch and of beer out of the bottle if the occasion calls for it, you can take her home to mom, she can make small talk, your dad will be jealous–he never had it so good–your friends will want her (she would never), she's witty but not clever, clever but never cute, she has an innate decorating know-how, knows which cutlery to use, and how to get stains out of shirts, she loves (or at least pretends, very well, to love) giving blow jobs and most important of all, boobs. Glorious boobs. Beautiful but firm bouncing boobs that go up and down and up and down, up down, up down and up. Just the right womanly way, all the way along the subway platform.

Man.

I want to be that kind of great guy-getting' woman.

Today we are alone in the subway-car and she is contemplating gas.

"Why do I fart so much?"

She can make anything hot. I swear to god.

"We're old, dude."

"Do I smell like poop: like a senior?"

She does–sometimes.

"You don't–never."

"You are sweet." She puts her hand on my lap. "But do not ever call me old. I am not lonely so *I* am not old."

LAVALIFE

Believe it: an over-active imagination leads to internet dating services.

It begins with variations on one question: why not me?; i.e., why her and not me; what are they, these happy nubile chicks, doing right and what am I doing wrong–not doing; what, how and why is *she* better, or her, or that one there; what's wrong with me; why don't I have a boyfriend when she does and she does?

All I see around me are couples. Couples in love. Couples happy. Couples horny. Couples holding hands in the park. Couples breaking up.

I even imagine how great it would be to break-up. I mean, the anguish—the sublime anguish like in Turner's painting, *A Slave Ship*—as you are told that you are being left—that you are being left for someone who is not better, you know. No not better. She's just got an ordinary job. Oh you know, it's nothing special. Just uh… just a dancer. Yeah. No. Not ballet. Stripper. And you realize you are being left for a sex-worker, a peeler, a fucking whore. And that maybe you really should have told him about those surprise plastic platform stilettos hidden in the liquor cabinet on his birthday and maybe you should have done that dance for him in your fine floss panties—with all the pole work and floor gyrating and fingering of your own anus. But instead you took him for Ethiopian and had sex by candlelight. God you're stupid! Stupid and boring.

That break-up anguish—shoulda woulda coulda, fuck you, I'm sorry. I didn't mean it. Take me back. I'm an idiot. And the…. Fuck you too! Followed by self-loathing.

And yes, I did compare my petty personal unrealized stripper dreams heart-break to a slave ship sinking, and no I am not sorry.

I'm sorry he didn't like me.

And that is how I ended up on Lavalife.

How's that going?

Nightmarish.

NIGHTMARE 1:

I dream.

I dream I am floating through a sky of faces. Scruffy fabulous five o'clock-shadow faces. Men heads detached from men bodies. And they are all trying to kiss me. But I just keep tapping them away and they float, float float float back into a an azure vanishing point. And another. And another. "You're all fabulous!" I say. "But you're not the one. Sorry." So much power. So much selection. Flick. "Bye. Bye.... Sorry."

When from the dusky distance, I hear, "What are you like 40?"

"What? Who said that?"

I turn around.

I'm in a grocery store. Pushing my cart down an aisle full of manikins. I've got a few in the basket already. But I want more. I'm hungry for manikins. The aisle goes on and on and on. Straight and forever with bad florescent lighting making everything flicker yellow. There are girl manikins on the left and boy manikins on the right. Everyone separated and stiff.

Like a grade seven dance.

Suddenly, Mike is across from me. He's my best friend. We talk every night. But now, across from me, he's a stranger–a different Mike–an alluring Michael. I want him only a daring arm's length away. Us in unison. Stamping side to side, i.e. dancing, in the gym.

Romance!

But he's just standing there stiff.

Where's my goddamn slow song–the special moment in the elementary school gym that smells like sweat-socks that will change my life... forever?

Where is Whitney Houston singing our song? For me. Me and Michael.

Oh my god!

"Didn't We Almost Have It All" *is* playing.

And, ohmygod ohmygod, Michael is walking towards me.

Holy Moly! I am controlling the world with my mind!

He's staring right at me, deep into my eyes, and he's rubbing the palms of his hands the way he does when he is nervous and he's getting closer and this is the best thing ever, I have ever felt. Michael getting closer.

And then, he deeks left.

When I look to my left, I see her in all her crop-top glory, Ann Marie–my best grade-seven girlfriend–taking Mike's hand. Mike's hand to dance. To dance to my Mike song.

"Didn't we almost have it all?" I'm gonna kick your ass Whitney Houston you crackhead bitch.

It's okay. It's okay I tell myself. They are a foot apart.

I am watching Ann Marie. I mouth, "I am watching you," when she looks over. Then, she moves in slow and close to Mike, so close and smooth, a groping palm on his ass.

Mike is really enjoying it. Damn her and her overdeveloped bosom. Damn her! Aren't there any goddamn chaperones at this kids' dance for the love of Christ! They're dancing like they have no arm gauging abilities. This is totally unacceptable. Pornographic almost. Finally, the Grade eight teacher Mr. Harrison yells at them. He looks like he should be gesturing. But he can't. He can't because he has no arms! Ann Marie's mom starts yelling at him and she wants to point but she can't because, she has no arms. My friend Ariel "The Leaner" Gonsalves has fallen and can't get up. She roles around on the gym floor like a hot greasy sausage out of its pan. What's going on? What's going on!?! I look down. Slowly.

My arms shrivel like two pricked balloons. Until....

A grocery cart trundles forward ahead of poor armless me. Everything on the shelves is soup. Cans of soup. Nothing but dented old dusty soup cans, aisle after budget aisle. My cart is totally empty. Who wants budget soup? LAME! I feel hard. Not hard of heart, actually I feel quite mushy on the inside. But hard on the outside. Like I have a shell. And not some metaphoric shell for my feelings like I know you are thinking. But like a real, for real shell. Something is not right. I catch a glimpse of myself in the reflective metal on my cart handle. And... and.... I can barely say it.... I am the worst kind of soup. The ultimate in budg' shit soups. *I... am Habitant Pea Soup!* Dear God.

And I hear a saccharine maternal whisper that seems a song in my subconscious: *Better watch those mushy thighs.*

Alarm! Alarm! Alarm!

NIGHTMARE 2:

For real. This is my real life everyday nightmare.

I am awake.

Very awake—on my fifth coffee this morning.

I'm at work.

I was late for the third time this week.

I measure my time in late days and coffee runs.

No one seems to notice.

No one notices me.

I have become the pallid portrait of 30-plus and female. My cubicle. I pretend to work. I surf my potential love life. *Niente.* The walls are grey carpet. No view out. My mouth tastes like my grade five math teacher smelt after break in the teacher's lounge: stale, acrid. I'm in a stale room that's not really a room. There's no colour. I look at my newspaper clipping of Einstein rustled by the aircon. Einstein had dates—a wife even. Pallor. I have no one to have dinner with, care for, care for me. An empty room but full of stuff, papers, pictures out of place, like when you first move in and the paint hasn't been picked, mixed, poured and then painted. An empty room until you pour the love in.

I check my Lavalife, again. No IMs. No hellos.

I get ready to leave work.

No one says good night.

It's raining out and no one told me. I don't have an umbrella or a jacket or anything. The heavy clouds just extend my office life into my life-life: grey. And when I step out from under the awning, it pours down on me.

Fuck you pathetic fallacy!

All I need is 100 cats to complete this—my portrait.

HELP ME SWEET CHARLIZE

"Help me Charlize."

Charlize bakes. That's her thing. Her other thing is that everything has to be equal. She believes that meaning exists between things. "It's all dynamics," she says. But I say the last thing about her is dynamic. She has only one chair that she keeps out of her room in case the bed gets jealous, one table, one lamp, no sofa (its girth threatens the chair). Everything is one colour. Everything. And she can never decide. Should it be macadamia or chocolate chip, gooey peanut-butter or melty melty fudge, rot-your-teeth-out shortbread or dollop of treacle, toffee, coffee, molasses "my own creation cookies" cookies? So she eats everything in equal parts right out of the oven, making Charlize like her cookies: sweet and round.

She's the kind of girl you can trust. And I do. And yes, I just said something terrible about the rotund. What a stereotype! But, said stereotype has me ready to contemplate a kitten book.

"There's this self-help book, *The Kitten Within*. I swear it'll help you with your dating life. It'll help you with the beginning of your new Lavalife."

She makes it sound like I am a character from a grade nine Latin text—a hapless Pompeii citizen happily living at the foot of Mt. Vesuvius and then....

"Yeah. I would lend you my copy but I already gave it to Daniella a while ago—like before you met her even. I should get that back one day. It worked for her—did it ever," Charlize says.

Bhengggggggggggggggg. (This is the sound of a dial tone. This is the sound of victory. This is the sound of me out the door. This is the sound of my future sex-life.)

47

I'm at the check-out of Chapters with my I-rewards card in one hand and a chartreuse book with kittens on it in the other and a dumb grin on my face.

The check-out girl asks, "Like, did you find everything you were looking for?"

I retort, "No. But I'm going to," and I hold the book up and shake it over my head–grin persisting.

"Um. Like okay then. Whatev'."

Little known fact: you can learn to play pool by reading. I did. I borrowed a book from the library and then schooled everyone's asses in my neighborhood. Made some mad cash too.

I plan to get a wealth of knowledge from *The Kitten Within*.

More importantly, if Daniella gets to "do it" from a book, so can I.

THOUGHT GEMS

The Kitten Within. I quote: "Too much seriousness can constipate an otherwise fluid situation." He, the author, one Craig Iano, is talking about dates. Yep. He's using a shit metaphor.

I'm at work. Reading. The computer's on my Lavalife home page. Einstein looks at me solemnly. He disapproves of my taste in literature and lifestyle.

I turn Einey over and read on.

On being in a relationship: "If you want to see how a cat works, and you cut it open to find out, you'll only end up with a dysfunctional cat." Am I wrong here? Doesn't that just make for a dead cat?

Well, I already have one of those. Baduh-bah!

Huh. This stuff is actually kinda making me happy.

Gem three: "Not everything needs vivisecting." Let me know if you think I am wrong here but, does anything *need* vivisecting?

Next, as if Craig has wire-tapped my brain, I read, "Don't analyze."

Okay. Alright. Maybe uh…. Maybe I do a little too much of that. Sure.

Craig Iano's crown jewel: "Don't analyze. Happy Hypothesize."

I'm good with happy, but Craig…. Happy hypothesize? What a load. Happy hypothesize! I want to scream this out loud. I open my mouth to laugh and–blewp. Huh? I made a high pitched "blewp." That can't be good. I'm pushing things aside in my purse to find a mirror to see what's wrong with my mouth. Blewp. And then, blewp blewp. I look around. Nothing. No one. People are typing. Blewp. Einstein?

I reach toward Einey. My screen is flashing. What? Wait. My screen is flashing. My Lavalife live messenger is flashing!

49

I start Happy Hypothesizing faster than an old Italian catholic lady speaks in tongues.

HappyhypothecizeHappyhypotheciszeHappyhypothecize. Thank you Craig Iano. HappyhypothecizeHappyhypotheciszeHappyhypothecize.

NOT QUITE BRIDGET JONES

My bacon strip is sizzling.

As soon as Scott Bloom agreed to meet me at the Vic for a pint, I ran as fast as I could from work, to the drugstore to home.

I get inside the door tear my clothes off and lather myself in Veet. Sweet sweet ammonia hair-removing relief.

I get my blow-dryer out. My make-up prepped to put on. I pick out a playful outfit–skanky really. Eat some chicken strips pre-nuked in the nuker two days ago. Let the hot water run in the shower. And, about twenty minutes later, decide now's a good time to see if this Veet stuff really works.

And it does. Really. Really work. Especially if you want to deeply exfoliate your anus and your labia.

At the Vic I am trying not to think of shit metaphors. I am trying not to think of vivisected cats. I am swigging back pints. On a positive note: I can't think. I can't over analyze a thing this guy is saying because I am trying so hard not to think of the pain in my pants.

"You've got a little something..." he touches the corner of his mouth.

I wipe my face.

"No. No. The other side."

I touch my face.

He chuckles, "No. Just a little down."

Sam from *Who's The Boss* had a crush on a pale-blue-eyed pre-college quarterback stud. He told her she had something on the corner of her mouth and it led to her first kiss. It was hot. Hot in a pre-teen kinda way. I think I want that. I'll show Scott Bloom who's boss.

And before I know what is happening I am running my hand from my mouth down toward... like I learned in salsa class when I pulled my calf muscle. Damn those colorful Puerto Ricans and their sultry dance moves.

I'm not sure at this point if I am drunk and need to check to see that my vag is still intact or if I am actually hot for this Scott Bloom guy, but after touching my pussy and feeling happy and also happy hypothesizing about it, the bill is paid and we're out one door, the restaurant, and in another, his place.

I don't really think I had looked at Scott before this. Not really. I'm not sure if I even have now. But I can tell you this, he has a bar fridge beside his bed. I ask you, does anyone older than twenty-five have a bar-fridge beside their bed? (And even then, is it ever okay?)

"How old are you? You didn't say on your profile."

"Does it matter?"

And now that he has my pants around my ankles, I guess it doesn't.

He looks up from my shins. He looks up from my shins and says, "Ooo." He says, "Oooo baby I like it raw."

I think I might be sick. I sit up. I sit right up and say, "I think I might be sick."

He puts a hand on my shoulder and says, "Here's some water. Just relax."

And I do. I relax right back and look at Scott Bloom. Scott Bloom is a trapeze artist and it shows. It shows in his eight-pack abs, and in his rock hard thighs and in his sinewy arms. Imagine being hoisted by Scott Bloom arms. I do. I do and it's good.

Scott reaches into his bed-fridge and pulls out a chilled bottle of absinthe.

"I can't...."

He puts his hand over my mouth. He runs the cold bottle down my body. This feels good. Then he rests it on my inner thigh and slowly moves the cool-green up to my hot-red. And this feels so good.

"Is it that bad?" I'm listless, embarrassed.

"It's pink. I like pink."

And before I have time to think about how lame what Scott just said is, he flips me over on my stomach and starts in for the rim-job.

I like this guy.

He only stops once to take a huge gulp of absinthe (Uh. Remind me never to take a drink from that bottle) and then his face is back, buried in my lovely lady-lumps.

God bless.

Then, there's this rumble. A deep rumble from within the Bloom. His chest is flush with my back. He's lunging forward. And back. And forward again. Like he's fucking me. But, I'm pretty sure he's not. And then, and then.... I feel something wet, wet and sticky trailing down my ribs. I know. Jizz. Right?

I look under my arm and see, what I see is Scott making like he's kissing my ribs but really, really he's gulping up the trail of green ferries he's purged all over my back. Translation: Scott Bloom is eating his own absinthe vomit off me.

AFTERMATH

After I add it all up, I want Scott back.

I call.

No answer.

It was sweet the way he tried to relax me.

I call.

No answer.

You have to give him credit. It's nice that he'd go to all that effort cleaning up his own mess that way. And his tensing biceps were… sweet.

Einey is having none of this. What would it be like to date a genius like Einstein? Would he fill you in on the secrets of the theory of relativity? Or would you be a constant source of embarrassment. Einey's ashamed of me—my lust. I can tell he's looking at me like I'm stupid. The up-side: Einstein probably looked at a lot of people like they were stupid.

I call.

I just want to make sure he's okay. I mean he probably feels pretty bad.

"Hi Scott."

He picked up.

"Oh hey."

"I just wanted to...."

"Oh. I think... scrshshshshh... we uh... scrshshshshh...."

He is actually making the scrshshshshsh sound with his mouth–not even paper.

"... we... scrshshshshh... have a bad connection."

Bhenggggggggggggggggg.

He. Hung. Up. I can't believe it.

I could give up here. I could take the hint. I could let go. Admit that getting drunk and trying to fuck someone much younger than me just makes me feel lonely–lonelier than I felt before. But I'm still kinda drunk.

I look at Craig's book. Its chartreuse a beacon in my cubicle grey-scape.

I'm thinking about kittens. Sex kittens.

It works for Daniella godamnit.

I pick up my phone.

It's got to work for me.

I dial.

This one is for me.

I figure: my new fake French accent is going to be the sound of my future sex-life.

Oh yeah. I'm calling subway Tim.

Suddenly, I don't feel so old.

HOW TO DATE A MEZZO

(Based on a true real-life story, from my true and real life.)

Opera singers may be hot, with their superhuman corset-inflated bosoms and their silky voices, but no good ever came from anything inflated and silky. Think Don King in a teddy: not to be trusted.

What to do in the unfortunate event that you are in an opera relationship:

1. ESTABLISH BOUNDARIES: How would you be if you were a woman with a voice that got you pants roles? I'll tell you: über-insecure. Mezzos are less secure than fresh-from-a-bender Lindsay Lohan trying to act next to Meryl Streep on a Chinese high-rise bamboo scaffold. So, Mezzos want to be good... good at everything. What does this mean for you? They want to tread on your creative turf. Whenever you turn your back or open your heart to an opera singer, they're going to try to one-up you. GAIN CONTROL. And fast. Here's what I said to my mezzo just last week after she sent me a playful and witty e-mail: Listen you two-bit opera hussy, I am the one who assumes various written identities here. That's why they are called I-dentities: they're mine. You don't see me wandering around in a chorus doing weird stuff, yeah, like pretending to talk to other people in the chorus (Don't think I didn't see you. Oh I did!) wearing a mammoth striped cotton ball on my head looking like

Blueberry Muffin.[1] (That's an allusion to Strawberry Shortcake.[2] That's right. I follow the series. What are you gonna do about it? I'll break your thumb.) So back off of my writing turf sister!

2. STAY FAITHFUL:

a) Mezzos are like magpies. If a stranger invades your nest and flirts with your opera singer, distract your little song-bird with some shiny beads. (Now, if your mezzo flirts with someone else, that's a different story: backhand her. No worries. You'll eventually recover from the high decibel caws.)

b) How do you stay true? At opera mixers, have a speech impediment handy. The natural snobbery of the opera singer will keep them at bay. However, you might find that an opera singer will be drawn to your speech impediment under a coy guise to help; naturally desperate for work as they are, they need to use those expensive diction classes of theirs any which way they can. In such a case, bark like a small dog. This technique is particularly helpful at avoiding contact with mezzos; they are jealous of anything that sounds soprano.[3]

3. SEX: Can you imagine how loud an opera orgasm is? In case of an opera orgy, bring head gear. The upside: nothing is hotter than

---

1 We all know, opera singers love their eats. Just the mere mention of food will abate any confrontation with one of their kind.
2 It's good to keep a bag full of deserts handy. You can use them for emergency mezzo control–like tallow sticks covered in peanut butter for a rottweiler.
3 Mezzo mantra: Why can't I be the pretty girl in the play? Why can't I be the pretty girl in the play?

a naked person with a speech impediment, barking like a dog while wearing orange plastic ear-muffs.[4] Hot!

4. END IT: If your mezzo wants to "move it to the next level" put your back-pack over your head and get as big as possible. Do not make eye-contact. Then back away from the opera singer as slowly as possible while speaking in dulcet tones. Leave an escape route for the opera singer. Get into your motor vehicle and drive, fast.

5. A BETTER WAY: Shoot the mezzo.

These five situational anecdotes should help you in your first relationship with any mezzo and, if you've followed along closely, in her last.

But remember the most important rule, avoid opera contact whenever possible.

---

[4] My current boyfriend requests this role play.

HOW COULD YOU HATE YOUR MOTHER? (LET ME TELL YOU)

A couple a months back I met this real peach of a guy.

I was telling him a bit about myself—about living all over South East Asia and coming back home to live with my mom. Right after I told him I was a vegetarian, he asks me, "You don't eat any meat?" I give him one sidelong glance. "No meat? Not any meat, not ever?" I recognize an invitation. I slide my hand up his inner thigh.

He is just the kind of sweet meat I need.

His name is Harry Bello. It's a grown man's name but he barely acts like he's nineteen. Suits me fine. I like him. He's an Italian stallion and I just want him to buck while I ride.

Giddyup!

But when I get back from the washroom, well, at first things are great, but then, he goes all soft on me—not literally—no one ever goes soft on me.

"Your ass is like steel" he says.

"Like steel?"

"Yeah I watched you walk away and… oof… it's like a terminator ass. It's killing me."

I nod my head towards his crotch and ask, "Did it move?" He looks clueless. I expand, "Did watching my ass make your cock stiff?" and I think he'll go on.

But he doesn't go on in that vein at all and that's the vein I want him to go on in.

Instead he starts to play with my hair and says, get this, "You're like a delicate flower."

"A delicate flower!?!"

I look like I just ate a salted prune.

Harry looks like he might swallow his tongue.

I feel him pull away. So I try to bring Harry back around, fast.

I put my hand under shirt and feel for his nipple.

"You wanna see this double-barrel ping-pong trick I learnt in the brothels of Bangkok. It's a hoot. If you like dirty tricks. Do you like things that are dirty, Harry?"

I see him shift his weight and grab at his pants; he looks intrigued.

I need this bad.

Asia isn't the land of milk and honey for straight white girls like me. I never caught yellow fever, but every guy I wanted to shag sure did dance to the tune of Bowie's *China Girl*. I didn't make any money.

I had to come back.

Back to Moms.

Me living at home works for her. I stuff my face with chips and listen to her talk about the extended history of malls: Dixie Mall, Sheridan Mall, the Eaton Centre. Most nights I listen, curled up on the couch. She likes to have something to talk at.

◎

Problem: I can't fuck Harry when Moms is around.

She hates it when I bring him over. The first time he wasn't even coming over, he just came to pick me up, and she yelled at me forever about how another man, a proper man, would come to the door. But I don't want a proper man.

I want Harry. When he comes over, it's not so bad being back with Moms.

Most times he and me we pretend we're watching a movie while she's busy with her DuMauriers and People magazine in the back room.

Still, I need more than fooling around. It's getting to me. He's just too fuckin' hot for dry humping in Levi's and finger-banging.

But I need my own space. Even for what we get up to.

It's pretty hard to keep quiet when Harry's kitkatting me and whispering in my ear about how he'd like to ATM.

I didn't even know what those things were until Harry did a little show and tell.

Harry told me, "A Kit Kat is a candy bar made up of four finger-sized chocolate covered biscuits." Then he put his four fingers together and crammed them down my pants. "And ATM does not mean Automatic Teller Machine. It means, Ass To Mouth. Get it? If not, just you wait."

Did I ever get it when he showed me. I'm surprised he didn't go deaf with the sounds coming out of me.

But I've got it under control. Not my noises. God, I couldn't have that under control with Harry. No, I've got the space thing under control.

Harry's best friend is heading out of town and taking his girl with him. She, I happen to know for a fact, needs someone to stay at her place. She's a swell girl with a good heart and a multitude of mirrors in her room. I can already see Harry perspiring and pounding away at me from behind x 8 POV. I dream of how he's gonna make me wet all over.

God!

I volunteer to water her plants.

Harry comes over the first night with some gin and tonic and wants to show me something on youtube. Yay. It's a UFC fight. Yeah, I'm not much into it but I'm willing–willing to do anything because he's so damn good looking. Still, after a few belts of gin and four hours of fight watching I'm done. But Harry's all revved up. He wants to wrestle.

Suddenly I'm awake–wide awake; I love touching Harry's body. What a body!

At one point he asks me to straddle him, put both hands on his chest and just grip. Normally I would just ask him to fuck me at this point but he's all serious about this wrestling stuff. He tells me that I have to look up–that the move only works if I look up. So there I am sitting on top of Harry Bello gripping his chest and looking up and I have never felt more like I am fucking someone but not really and I can feel his chest under my hands and my hands are so small on his chest and just when I am so sure he can feel how hot my pussy is on his stomach, he flips me face down onto the ground and drills his knee into my back.

"Ooo. I like being submitted," I say.

He asks, "You do?"

I bat my eyelashes once and twice and before I can say anything he's offering me his hand to help me up.

Deep inside, I'm rolling my eyes.

And after we've wrestled—wrestled for an hour on the floor—he wants to talk. And we do. About whatever he wants: Serra, Georges St. Pierre, the many differences between Boxing, Kickboxing, Jujitsu, Judo, Greco-Roman wrestling, Tae Know Do. I'm all ears. He's just about to explain what MMA and UFC have in common when he says, "You look worn out."

I am.

"I guess I better let you get some sleep."

And we're both standing there in the kitchen not wanting him to leave. Or, at this point maybe it's just me. Maybe I just don't want him to leave. But we're standing there and I say, "Bye, I guess."

He turns away.

And I want to cry 'cause Harry's leaving me with nary a finger fuck.

And then, out of nowhere, he turns back and he does this thing—this thing I think I've seen in Disney princess movies where the Prince Charming presses his lips together really hard, leans his head in—he leans his head in to me real slow and closes his eyes, tight. I—I don't know what else to do so I do the same and the result is... is a peck—a peck goodnight.

I'm confused.

He was the guy all over me, right? That guy who just left, he's the guy who told me to climb in the back seat of his car to lick the cream out of his cannoli? Am I right?

I don't get it.

I just don't get it.

Is that what regular girls call a date?

Maybe I went on a date. I. Went. On. A. Date.

I've struck romance gold!

Harry Bello is hard *and* soft. Like a Caramel bar right out of the refrigerator. Hard and dark, but how do they get that saccharine softness inside? Harry, he's a sweet complex mystery.

I like this. I decide to like this new Harry. It makes me want him more.

I'm thinking this over–thinking about my Bello, the Astroglide I had stashed by the bed for Harry all over my fingers and my hand down my pants–when the phone rings.

It's Moms.

"Well your father doesn't understand why you didn't take that insurance job and neither do I. You must be a very privileged kind of person with debt. I have debt and...."

I want to yell at her, "It's past two you ol' hag. Go to sleep already and give the rest of us some... rest!"

But I think about Harry–Harry in control of my body. About Harry having me on the floor–literally. I imagine him pinning me down and asking me to do wrong things to myself. And I feel too good.

I stuff the phone under a pillow and just pretend Moms is in the other room. I try and carry on where I left off–amusing what I think of as my Bello bits. But I can hear her natter, endlessly. If I hang up she'll call back. Or, worse, she'll show up–talking. Until what feels good, feels dead.

And I give up. And pick up the phone, and listen.

◎

When I hear Harry's friend and his girl are coming back, I hurry to ask Harry over.

As soon as he's there, Harry turns on the computer. I think it's going to be just another UFC and me mad-attempt at masturbation night. But when Harry asks me to go to this site to help him to choose something, I start to feel all gooey inside–like I matter–like how I feel matters to him.

"So which picture of me do you like?"

Ahhhh. Sweet Harry.

I take a long time explaining what I think each picture of him means. And then I settle on one where I tell him he looks like a really tough artist or something.

"If you know what I mean."

Harry says, "Yeah."

And I'm dying inside, just dying, 'cause he knows what I mean. And maybe 'cause he knows that, maybe now, I hope, he knows how much I want to fuck him.

Harry puts his hand on my shoulder and looks me straight in the eyes. I take a deep breath in. The way he's lookin' at me, I feel like something just dropped inside of me.

The bomb: "I think maybe I'll blow that picture up for Lena then."

Lena's Harry's ex. Oooo. She's a soprano. Oooo. Whatever. I hear sopranos are a dime a dozen.

But Harry just won't shut up about goddamn Lena.

"Oh. Lena was so funny last night; she was on fire! We went for ribs and she did this thing. She bites a small whole in her creamer and makes like she's milking a cow. It's great. You gotta see it. And then when we were leaving, I mean you know Lena–I mean Lena–she's a cute girl. So we're leaving and this punk sez to her, 'Hey shorty, what's it cost?' like she's a whore right. And I say, 'For you guy? Four teeth,'" and Harry snorts and slaps his knee. "Four teeth!"

He looks at me.

"Well Lena thought it was pretty good."

"Good for Lena."

I'm sure everything is *great* for Lena.

When I walk Harry to the door, Harry goes through the same routine from the time before. The lean in, the closed eyes and the puckered lips for a kiss goodnight.

I close the door.

It's a kiss goodbye.

◎

I'm coming in the door and Moms is putting the food on the table.

I throw my bags down and lie on the couch and she starts to talk.

This is why I hate her.

It's not the time she flirted with my counselor after my anorexia pass-out in the halls at school by quipping, "As soon as I heard, I came when I could." Hahahaha-*ha*.

It's not the time she said, "Can't you see I'm on the phone? Well, it takes two to tango dear," after daddy had left strangle marks lined around my neck and a welting, would-be black eye for punctuation.

It's not even now, when the first thing she says is, "Why buy the cow if you can get the milk…" and I want to scream, "I didn't even get to be his milk. I didn't even get to be his goddamn milk," and cry.

It's when we sit down to dinner and everything is quiet and she looks at me and says, "I'm glad you're home."

HOW TO DATE A WRITER

1. Don't.

2. I highly recommend against it.

3. Avoid it at all costs.

4. You are still not listening to me are you?

5. Fine.

6. Fine.

7. Just do whatever you want. It's your broken heart in the end, what do I care?

8. Sure you like it now but just wait....

9. What's that? You need my shoulder to cry on? Well, I told you not to.

10. You're right. You're right. I never told you why not to.

11. Turn the page.

HOW TO DATE A WRITER

DON'T![1]

---

[1] You're still with the writer!?! Well, I thought you might take me more seriously what with the bigger font. Uhh. Okay. Yes. I'll tell you why not to. Turn the page.

Do you feel cheaply manipulated yet? Well if you date a writer you will. I did, and I am still in therapy.

HOW TO DATE A WRITER[2]

1. **IS THERE ANYTHING LESS SEXY THAN WRITING?** Sure there is, like picking your nose or reading, or picking your nose while you are reading. But as an art form can you think of anything less sexy? Writers can't. Pablo Picasso had chicks fight over him while he was painting. Actors get pussy handed to them on a platter.[3] And, c'mon, who hasn't given Pete Townshend a blow-job backstage? But no writer, ever, has gotten laid by asking someone to come home and watch them type.[4]

Or how about this: guitar guy as proof positive that writers are unsexy. You go out. Your friends meet up with other friends. You're all drinking Jack. You get to talking to the cute guy who hasn't had a decent meal or haircut in ten years and his primary fashion source is Value Village and you agree to go to the Matador and drink 'til 8 a.m. and then when he gets you home and after you drink some more and he's gotten you into his room... he whips out the guitar. You sleep with him right?[5] It's kinda charming. You kinda wanna see how those quick fingers operate south of the border. Slot a writer in there instead. Based on the success of every guitar guy

---

2 Subtitle: A writer is born.
3 Bon appétit!
4 Trust me. I've tried so many times.
5 He could sing Cumbiya for three hours and you'd still let him munch your box (if only to shut him up.) Wouldn't you? (I did.)

that has lulled me into a state of affection with their dreamy tunes, I decided that when I got someone home after hours of imbibery,[6] I would beguile him with a poem—my po-em—from my chapbook of po-eh-try. I haven't been laid in three years.

Writers are the bottom of the art/sex barrel[7] and they know it. If "Do you really want me? (Do you like my writing?) Me? Are you sure? (What did you think of chapter 3?) You're sure it's me you want? I'm not sure that it's me you want (Why don't you ever like what I write?)" seems like foreplay to you, then you are almost ready to date a writer.

2. GOD COMPLEX. Who knows more than a writer? No one. That's because of all the research they have to do for their writing.[8]

You may be a tennis pro but I just wrote a book with a subsidiary character who was the tennis coach to Maria Sharipova[9] and so I actually know more about the game than you ever could. Like, did you know that the term love for zero actually comes from the French *l'œuf* meaning egg, which, of course, looks just like zero? Oh you did know that. Well. Hmmm. Actually I don't think tennis is right for you anyway. You'd make a better mommy. It's all the rage. You should just get pregnant.

Being demeaned is a big part of loving a writer. Sound good yet? Just wait 'til we get this party started.

---

6 Only a fucking wankey writer uses a word like that.
7 Art/sex barrel rated a worse place to be than the Pickle Barrel.
8 Substitute surfing porn for research and masturbatory smorgasbord for writing and you'll know why writers actually spend hours in their offices.
9 Man did I do a lot of deep research and hard writing on her.

3. WHO LET THE BIBLIOPHILES OUT—WHO! WHO-WHO!?! No seriously. Who let these fuckers have a party? Can we even call it a party? I don't know about you but the last time a big group of us sat around listening to one person read we called it preschool, not party. And sure like at a real party there's always one middle-aged guy in the corner trying to pick-up an "eighteen year old," but everyone else is just a shuffle of perspiring pompous awkward clotted together next to the bar–hovering nervously. Which brings me to my next point, not even beer helps these people. Hell! Hard liquor can't help them. Nothing can help an animal that has been locked in its fluorescent-lit cage for days on end to come out and socialize. Writers are essentially the same as tech-geeks without the brains or complimentary salary. At least the tech-geeks have the decency to stay indoors playing *Starcraft II*. But, because writers like to pretend they are cool, you'll be forced to these parties or launches, as writers like to call them. You'll be subjected to awesome jokes like, "Giving birth to that post-modern piece made me post-partum" or, "Oh. Jordan. Reading that Foucault is more like joining a *fou* cult." That high school girl in the corner with the fifty-year old drooling down her cleavage, she's starting to look like the lucky one, yeah? Do you want to kill yourself yet? I know I do. But that's because I am a writer and as such...

4. ... I CAN BARELY KEEP THIS RAZOR-BLADE OFF MY WRIST. Pharmaceutical companies were invented as a writer help-line. Think Sylvia Plath or Anne Sexton. Think Hunter S. Thompson or Truman Capote.[10] And those are the successful ones.[11] Imagine how much

---

10 What's that you say? Truman Capote didn't kill himself. Well maybe he should have since I think he did.
11 So, think about how suicidal I must feel.

better they could have been on Prozac, Zoloft, or Wellbutrin–how much more they could have written, said and done. Imagine the great literary contributions we have been robbed of due to depression.[12] Thank you Pfizer. So, in this modern age, you may not have to walk in on your lover with his or her head in the oven but you will be a big help in classifying, categorizing and dispensing your lovers happiness cocktail. You'll also be a big help if you are really quiet when they are sprawled out on the couch watching TV in their underwear "working." It may look to you like they are just a lazy unemployed fat-fuck lying on the couch but this is actually where the magic happens. The couch is actually an inspiration mobile. Dr. Phil is a dream weaver. And the lack of clothing is a uniform designed to liberate the mind–*my imagination engine*. The ketchup chips? Those are just ketchup chips. Oh and could you straighten-up around here it's getting hard to think with all the mess.

You want out right? Well you can't have out. I need you. I need you. If you leave I will kill myself.

And just when you think you have replaced my mood-stabilizers with enough sugar pills to help gravity bring that sharp edge to a major artery, spurts of blood alerting you of your freedom–psyche! I'm not gonna kill myself silly. We're both still here, together.

5. ENDING IT. It never ends. There's this little game I like to play. It really gets me in touch with the theatrical roots of my poetic soul. Kay. Stand there. Ah. Ah. Ah. Who said you could exit stage left? Did I say you could exit stage left? Now I know I didn't tell you you

---

[12] This is only possible if you can imagine hard enough to believe that anyone reads.

could exit stage right. I told you to stand there and stay. Good, now do that until I say you can go. If you go before I say you can go, I will.... I will.... I will write you a plethora of melancholy e-mails and letters. And, if you don't answer, well, I'll write a story about you in which I publish all your old e-mails to me, grammatical errors and typos and all, and I'll just call you Nyler instead of Tyler so that everyone knows how pathetic you are. What? I'm pathetic. How could you call me that? It's just that I love you so much. I love you more than anyone ever could. I love you more than a thousand love poems written by a mutation hybrid Shakespeare/Donne poet could ever write. What? You'll stay. Sweet! I win again.

6. WHAT'S TO BE GAINED? If all of that sounds good to you, than you are ready to date a writer. And, if you are lucky, you might just get so fucked over and so fucked up that you need to write a novel about it all... and see a shrink for the next six years.

JULIUS CAESAR: A PLAY REVIEW

This play was pretty good but God! that guy obviously never took a playwriting class. All the best stuff happens at the beginning. I mean who really cares what happens in a play called *Julius Caesar* after the title character dies? And, like, Mark Antony, Brutus, and Cassius aren't as cool. They just aren't. I'm sorry. I mean who has even heard of them? Not I.

Who I have heard of is Margaret Atwood. And that's really what I was there to see: the master herself. She was there—two rows down from yours truly: me, an M.A. long-time admirer.

The show, it was über-pc, a first-nations interpretation—an easy pill to swallow so the who's who of the old-biddy blue hairs was out. I'm NOT claiming here that the queen of CanLit is a blue-hair, just that Margaret goes to their soirees. They're her people. No. No. I definitely do not think she's "old." I see her another way. The blue-hairs may be her crowd—read Madame Atwood—but she's so beyond that. So beyond time and the age thing.

Anyway, reading her is for the agèd's own good; it may be the last good thing they read on this earth. I mean can you imagine, there you are, poised like Miss Havisham in your chaise-longue, your hard-earned thick drapes blocking out the blinding winter light, reading. When, suddenly, it grips you: Death. You float your frail way up, up to the pearly gates and there's Peter reading the *New York Times Magazine*. He asks you but one question: "What was the last book you read?" You answer with dignified dignity, *"Bear."*

And there's a snap. The trap door's out beneath you, you're on your way to Hell. You barely have time to gasp, "But it won the Governor General's Award!" And Peter looks down upon you, pity on his face as your feet start to singe, and he says something you never thought you'd hear from a saint, "That must have been in one of the Council's high years. You shoulda read *A Handmaid's Tale*. Or at least followed a steady diet à la Atwood. Goddammit! She's good."

So, on Peter's advice, I decide to just follow Margaret Atwood.

When she comes into the reception, she bee-lines it for the hors d'oeuvres tables. I shadow her and write down everything she eats. If I'm gonna train to be a writer I need to know *the diet*.

Strangely, she hits up the food table, filches one of everything and then takes-off.

But where to? Where did Margaret Atwood go with her plunder?

My bet's on the washroom. I bet if I went down there right now and opened the last stall there would sit little Maggie A., knees to her chin, covered in crumbs. I'd tell her it was alright. "It's okay Maggie A. I understand. You wanna smoke?" I would promise her, "Tomorrow, I will so make you my friend on Facebook Mags." And then Maggie and I would eat some *crudités* while smoking and gabbing about boys.

I might even tell her about my Spain dream. We'd tour together going from gala to reading gala the world over. But in Spain, in Spain....

Yeah. Me and Maggie Atwood flying on a pink champagne plane to a taffee ball in Madrid. I'm going to bring seven of my best money-dresses and my shoes made of coins. Maggie A. will have twenty and better. *Click-clack. Click-clack.* That's the sound our shoes make when we trod on the backs of the gypsy kids. To think. They, get me, me and Maggie A. to break their feeble spines! Ah. Lucky gypsy kids. Brings a tear to my writerly eye. What fun we would have–reading, drinking, demeaning.

She loves the dream! She gives me a little nod. She thinks I'm alright. Maggie stands up, lets me brush the morselletes from her petite, taut body, takes my hand in hers and guides me out–out of the washroom, out the doors of Buddies in Bad Times, out onto the street and out, on a cloud, into the dark night air.

Yeah. Julius Caesar's good.

But Margaret Atwood, now she's cool.

BUN HEAD

She sure is no bun head.

She's a modern dancer. She's art stream at our school. She's cool.

And my friend. My best friend Anya.

She's Russian which is also cool. But she hides it from the other girls. Only I know. Also cool.

She lets me know because I won't judge her, won't call her KGB or Ivan "I will break you" Drago–a natural enemy to us all. I never would.

I like her.

She sends me letters. I send her some back. She tells me things.

I know her dad gets a porn channel and her mom's mad about it, and I know there's a girl Kirsela in her class who smokes and sticks her fingers down her throat even though she didn't eat all day and then she can still dance for like a whole six hours after. And I know we both love *Grease*. Olivia Newton John is the best.

I tell Anya, I'm gonna get pants just like Olivia in the finale–tight and black and shiny.

We think this is a riot.

We also think it's a riot that one of the pretty girls in the movie sends her boyfriend perfumed letters. "Oh my God! What does a letter need perfume for: it isn't gettin' any!?!"–is our joshy-joke.

We sing, "You're the one that I want. Ooo. Ooo. Ooo. Honey. The one that I want," and she shows me some of Olivia's dance moves.

I can never get them right.

Anya says, "You have no rhythm," and laughs.

So we practice. We're practicing for the school dance.

We practice every night that Anya doesn't have to go to night-dance after dancing at school all day, which are only some nights. Anya says I need way more time but that she can whip me into shape for the dance no problem.

But now, I think we might not even get to do the finale dance–rhythm or no rhythm.

I sent Anya this letter about this guy in math class who rubs his hands in his pants and smells his fingers any time we are doing a spot-quiz. I wrote her all the gross details I know she would like. Like how he even takes those same fingers to squeeze a puss filled zit on his face or how he likes to touch everyone on the arm–oooo! butt arm. GROSS!!! And I took the letter to my grandma's house and doused it in Anais Anais and wrote, "PS Enjoy the smell of my sweet anus anus."

Anya got mad.

"It wasn't even in front of the bun heads. I wouldn't have cared if it were in front of the bun heads," she says. "Those ballet girls wouldn't have cared."

Apparently, when baited with cheap perfume, a drove of modern dancers becomes like a pack of hungry wolves. When Anya opened her bag in the change room and Anais Anais wafted into the air, they got a hold of the letter and pounced.

"Are you some sort of Dyke?"

"Have you been checking out my ass this whole time Anna? Do you want to stick your tongue in my pussy?"

And the real knock was at me–her with me.

"Anna! You're hanging out with a G level? Oh Anna...."

Cool girls can be so cruel.

"Well I didn't tell you to carry the f'n letter around," I cry.

I cry and cry so much that I almost choke.

"I know," she says. "I know."

"What now Anya?"

One of the girls set her up with her brother for the school dance. Anya looks real nice all in a dress and her hair done and stuff. The guy can't dance though; he's even worse than me. And Anya smiles but I can tell she's feeling awkward. He's got no rhythm but even she couldn't teach him.

I'm lurking like a kidnapper in the corner. I'm a creep.

I think maybe when they play my request Anya will look over. But when "Grease Lightning" comes on she doesn't even glance. She's like a jewelry box bun-head in front of a mirror; she only looks at herself.

Most of the time that's how it is even at school: I'm a gross creep and she's a tiny selfish dancer.

It's no fun.

But when she calls me, crying, I still answer. I answer like a dumb sap. Maybe her dad won't let her go out past midnight. Maybe her dad hit her mom. Maybe she got a B in technique. Whatever. I come when she calls.

All I know is, after all this, she owes me.

"You owe me one Anya," I say.

◎

I get my license.

Everyone will be there but Anya keeps her promise and comes to the roller rink with me anyway.

Man can Anya skate. Not one stumble.

"You're way better than Kirsela," I whisper in her ear.

Anya goes stiff as a board—as stiff as a board can go on eight wheels.

"You're way better than Kirsela," I say again.

"She's got great technique."

"It doesn't matter," I say.

"What you do looks better. More natural. You're a natural," I say.

She almost smiles.

I take her home in my brother's beater.

I know she's there beside me. I can feel it. The space between us is full and empty all at once—like dead air between double-pane windows.

I keep my eyes on the road.

She won't say anything.

It's like I forced her to come out.

"You're better. No question!" like I'm a broken record.

You owed me, I think.

I jerk the car at every stop. Anya doesn't even care.

You owe me more than this.

We get to her place and I'm thinking what to say. Nothing.

"I should go," I say.

I feel like I'm locked in a car with a stranger—a stranger who hates me.

Anya says outta nowhere, "Just come inside for a quick sec."

I look at her with squinty eyes. I got a million questions—a million things I'd like to say to her. I'd like to give her a piece of my mind. Maybe define friendship for her. Like maybe in Russian it means something different. I wanna say so and be a big time asshole...

"Come on!" she says. "I got you something."

... but I can't be an asshole. Anya makes me weak.

Her house is dark.

I never told Anya, not even in one of our letters and I guess now I never will: I'm afraid of the dark.

She's heading to the basement. I can hear her feet on the linoleum. My feet are much heavier–they make a heavy stupid sound.

"I don't know where to go Anya," I try not to make this sound like a plea.

I trip on the top stair but Anya catches me by my shirt. She goes down slowly. And holds my hand. Step by step.

She slides onto the cool leather of the couch and pulls me beside her. I can feel the goose bumps on Anya's skin.

This is weird.

I hear rustling. A soft paper package lands in my lap.

"Thanks Anya."

She gets up and turns on the TV. Before it warms up, I can't see anything.

I tear at my present. Shredding it–blind. My hands are shaking.

She's right beside me breathing.

I can hear her.

I can feel her. Watching. Calm.

I can feel the satiny smoothness in my lap.

My heart is racing.

She says, "They're black. Black tight pants."

Cool.

So so so so cool.

The TV is on her dad's channel. I look at Anya. I look at Anya. She has the volume turned way down. Everything is dark around us. I can see her chest go up and down–slowly.

I watch her for a while.

Then we both turn to the TV.

We stare straight ahead into the flickering light–into the fucking. Sitting still. Staring. Saying nothing.

But it's like we can hear each other.

And it's like we can see each other.

Without looking. Without listening.

Anya and me.

Breathing.

We finally fall into perfect pace.

Breathe.

Breathe.

Breathe.

CENTERFOLD

PERFECT ONLY WHEN TIMED RIGHT[1]

---
[1] Turn page.

SNATCH!

ALWAYS HUNGRY AND NEVER TASTELESS[2]

---
[2] Turn page.

MY

SNATCH

I AM AMERICA (AND SO CAN YOU!): A BOOK REVIEW

Fuck me senseless Stephen Colbert.

Oh. My. God! Silly me. Did I just say that out loud?

Before Stephen, there was Conan O'Brien. But that was just one of those school-girl crushes. You know. I had a few too many fuzzy navels at the frat one night and back at my U of T grad school dorm room me and my roommate got a little crazy just hitting each other with pink pillows, wearing oversized OHL[1] jerseys. We were just giggling, giggling, giggling ('cause that's what I, as a hot, naïve, juicy puck-bunny do up here in Canadia) when we got too close to the TV. Wham! It was all so fast. There he was, Conan. Or was... it... just a really funny 6' 4" shaft of light–like a late-night seraphim? And I was like, "That's *hot*!"

Whatever!

I don't even really remember it 'cause I was tipsy. So it doesn't even count–just like blow-jobs don't either. Know what I mean?

All I know is you college boys are all like sarcastic and smart and stuff. And now that I like books because I have learned to read them, I can tell you're really good Stephen. Really really... good.

---

1 Go Saginaw!

Stephen, you were, like, my first. I mean, Ohmygad! *I Am America (and So Can You!)* Does it get better? It's my first book so, like, really, does it? Well, I'll say no because, I mean, by page three I was peeing myself. I just can't wait to get to page four! I don't know what crazy things it'll make my body do. Oh my! Can you just imagine?

So here's my plan. I plan to get all this glory and fame from these reviews I keep writing and when Stephen has me on his show (I'll do satellite Stephen but trust me, you'd appreciate my talents much more in a personal interview.) I won't be as low-brow as that Hanoi Jane. I guess feminist has nothing to do with feminine because Fonda's no lady. She's a bitch. I won't be like her, Stephen. I won't sit in your lap. Or deafen your one good ear with my tongue. No! I'll respect your Catholic boundaries. I'll just dream into your dreamy brown eyes while you talk about politics or whatever and it may sound like the soundtrack for Charlie Brown's parents in my head, but don't worry my attention won't falter. And behind what may seem like a vacant creepy glare, which is really, a vacant creepy glare, I'll be thinking, "Stephen. Oh Stephen you're so smart. I bet all the book learning in the world couldn't make me as smart as you." But you'll tell me I'm cute and ask how did such great reviews come out of such a pretty little head like mine. And then, instead of shaking my hand you'll bow gallantly and kiss my fingers. Ahhhh....

See. That's all I want: a little on-air good clean Catholic fun.

And then maybe we can meet backstage after and you can teach me what it means to be American; you can show me what a Southern accent sounds like. And I'll say, "Wow! That's a sexy accent Stephen," and ask, "So Stephen. You're always taking about Catholic this and

Catholic that. What does it all really mean?" And you'll instruct me about the position of the virgin in Southern family values via Catholicism; i.e. you'll show me what Mary Worship means by kneeling at my altar.

It'll be great fun! I promise. I'll even incant, "It's a damn fine book Stephen. Damn fine. Oh. **Oh.** *Oh.* Stephen! What a big head you have. Oh my. Stephen, smart Southern men do eat better beaver!"

Whadaya say Stephen: will you teach me?

Loyally yours,

The True North strong and free (emphasis on free; as in, I'm really free).

PS Getting through my Master's without knowing how to read was really hard at first. It took a lot of fervent physical determination and training. In the end, I excelled at delivering orals in group seminars. Can I show you how I did it Stephen? Please. Can I please show you my expertise in dealing with big, hard, higher learning? I won't let you down, Professor Colbert. Cross my heart.

THE GLAD GARBAGE-BAG MAN: A PSYCHOLOGICAL PORTRAIT IN FILM

It's easy to coo and caw and wonder in awe about the passionate celebs of our time. Jess Simpson is like a well cut diamond in the sun–refracted light in a thousand rays coming from without and within: captivating! Especially while soapy wet and gyrating like a hood ornament on fuck-vibrate while wearing daisy dukes. *Talent classique!* And golly what a ride! But my true passion is for less formal talent–it's for the truly mediocre. For people with "talent" who end up in schmuck jobs on par with my own, which is answering the phone for eight hours a day. Yep. It's those poor dopes who went to Humber, George Brown or even Julliard to study the ancient art of drama only to begin and end their careers as Pokeroo or worse, as part of a touring children's theatre company. It's the crippled soul–the I need cash so bad I will sell my blood and let people experiment on my body–please give me this gig, god I need it bad, please. I'll be your cream cheese angel lady, your Mr. Clean. I'll even be your Maytag Repair Man. And I'll do it for pittance or bread, and bread at this point is probably better than pittance, please. Make no mistake, I'm not talking fallen from fame. No no. I'm not talking the hodge podge of eighties failed rock stars in the vein of Frozen Ghost.... Never heard of them? Oh well you can go down to the Gem and ask the once famous bartender all about it. He'll love you for it. I mean, why wouldn't he love to hear about his fall from grace while feeding boozy swill to alky swine that yell out, "I said bring me my Molson Ice, Glass Tiger!"

But I digress.

My raison d'être is to know these failed people–to know who they are underneath the commercial self, the physical embodiment of product. Their flagrant desire for more and their stifled acceptance of less. Their rise which is more like a blip and their fall which is more like a tumble down a ditch into that *je ne sais quoi* of, "Hey aren't you that guy?" guy-dom.

Glad Man:

1. What better way to know a fledgling actor than by the first film he owned. For the Glad Man it was when he was walking down 7th Ave after a particularly tough Method class and he saw it there in all its iridescent oil spill motif splendor: *Tron*.

Yes. Yes. *Tron,* you are so right when you say on the other side of the screen, it all looks so easy. On the other side of the screen there are no scene stealing Chaz's. No Marie-Paule's with foreign accents and exotic allure, drinking wine with the instructor after class. There is no adversary that you can't beat in the Light Cycle Arena with the help of a really sleek, sexual fantasy girl like Yori.

At night Glad Man inserts *Tron* into his VCR and thinks of Kimmy, his girl back home. Oh Kimmy. Sweet Kimmy and Yori have so much in common–a love of strawberry milk and good clean Christian non-judgmental anus tonguing. And as Glad slips into sweet orgasmic unconsciousness he moans about Wakachi, Idaho, and dreams about making it to the right side of the screen: "I'm coming for you Yori. I mean Kimmy. I'm coming just for you."

2. *Roxanne.* Why? Premature grey brotherhood. That's right. Just like Steve Martin, Gladdy was an early blooming silver fox. Why else? Kimmy just can't take the distance anymore and Glad needs a sliver of hope. If a middle aged man with a big nose can woo the hottest bitch in town, our Gladdy thinks he has at least a chance at getting Kimmy back to riding on the Gladdy-track. Little does he know that this classic tale of mistaken identity, inner beauty, and serenade induced, "Dear God man! why did you pan away from Daryl Hanna pre-op" hot sex-scene is so full of shit that after I watch it my asshole bleeds for days. But I guess if you're too much of a pussy to get what would really bring you hope at the video store, i.e., *Old Men Like High school Girls With Monster Tits, Roxanne* will have to do.

3. Glady gets what he really wants: *High School Girls Strip For Me Porn Sex Fuck Tits.* For some reason the poor grammar doesn't bother Glad. But nothing much bothers him anymore. Not that bitch Marie-Paule or Chaz or any of the kids in class. Not the homework for class. Not the size of his apartment. Not replacing the burnt-out bulbs or fixing the crack in the window. Or the abundant amount of towels, gym socks and crumpled tissues amassing themselves around his permanently terry-robed couch-bound body. What's your call: is this bountiful bliss or dour depression (the line is so blurry sometimes)? Mr. Glad Man's call is to Jenni. Or, Sisi. Or, Stacy, Candi, Tulla and Debbie. With a peppering of drunk'n'dials to Kimmy that result in marriage proposals of, "If in fifteen years neither of us is married...." followed by abrupt dial tone.

Oh sweet sweet singledom.

4. *Stepford Wives (1975):* Really Gladdy was looking for *Scrubba Dub Dub: Retro Housewife's Do It in a Big-ass Tub* but he grabbed the wrong vid off his friend's self. This flic was it. A Glad pivotal moment. Robot ladies are hot. Robot ladies who fake orgasms and keep home at the same time are extra hot. "How can I get me a piece of that homey action?" he thought. And he thought hard and he thought long. And he thought long and thought hard about how exactly he could fuck a chick from behind while she picked up his mess. And he came up with the wheelbarrow pre-swiffer jizz-powered lady carpet sweeper. Thanks to his Stepford adoration the list went on: the beer bitch; a three-foot tall flat-headed toothless woman with a penchant for standing very very still no matter what happens; topsy-turvy mop-a-top; sort of a three-dimensional naked Katherine wheel with a bucket and mop that operated on the theory that nothing got a floor cleaner than human hair; and finally, the backpack heeled-lawn aerator replete with mammary ear warmers–better known as the pokey-poke pussy pack.

Ah. The mother of invention really is need, desperate desperate need.

5. He got a job. He cleaned up and found Jesus. He keeps a trunk of filmic inventions in the garage. For every "Don't get mad. Get Glad!" he tells himself there is a difference between repression and subversion; helping women was all he had ever wanted– doing the right thing, lending a helping hand, those are what make a glad man. And for every piece of garbage that gets carried away and for every sandwich that is protected with airlock, Gladdy feels like a shoulder to cry on, a hand to hold. But when he watches *Predator* on his flat-screen in his high-rise bachelor

condo, he's mesmerized by Anna coming to pick up rippling bloodied heroic Arnie in a chopper and can't quite figure out why he thinks it's so cool. He doesn't think about the hunter becoming the hunted. He doesn't think about Kimmy. He doesn't think of acting school or New York. And he doesn't fall asleep to movies anymore. He thinks, "Why bother when you are living the dream?"

ARE YOU DATING A MAN READY FOR MIDDLE-CLASS MARRIAGE?

Testimonial: I thought my boyfriend and I were headed for nowhere. I was really sad about that. Thanks to this quiz, when he wouldn't get me an Asscher cut engagement ring, I realized I was crazy to stay with him. He realized that that was crazy too. So, he mortgaged his parent's 300 year old Muskoka cottage and instead got me the Princess cut. Can anyone say *upgrade?* All thanks to this quiz!

The truth shall set you free. Answer these questions directly and I promise you the truth:

1. When you go out does he show up
    a. on a bike
    b. in an SUV or old-model SAAB (seat warmers a must)
    c. in a minivan he already owns so that he can take his friend's son's soccer team to practice
    d. in a Smartcar[1]

2. One or both of you
    a. work at BMO
    b. use words like BMO and pronounce them B-moe
    c. drink Soave and insist on calling it So-ah-vey instead of Swah-vey
    d. drink 50 and pronounce it fitee[2]

---
[1] Small cars carry big brains. Run away. This guy may be an academic–definitely no money.
[2] Small town northern Ontario alert! Hick alert! Hick alert eh!

3. Has he ever
    a. used the word giver
    b. used the expression giver berries
    c. chosen the colour Crisp Berry for his dining room walls
    d. asked you to lick his berries after he comes in from a run

4. The last time you had sex was when
    a. he demanded it
    b. he waited patiently for it
    c. he begged for it and then you gave him head instead because you were tired after company baseball but that was what he really wanted in the first place[3]
    d. you begged for it, he closed his eyes and pumped

5. What kind of porn does he watch?
    a. barely legal
    b. barely legal boys
    c. under the mattress and on visible computer files: anal play with big breasted babes[4]
    d. he doesn't watch porn[5]

---

3 No more. He is so ready for middle-class marriage. Congratulations!
4 In his hockey bag or between his woodworking mags you find Freshmen and your old copies of Playgirl. (Total marriage material girl!)
5 Ka-reepy!

6. Does he look like this[6]

7. Have you finally trained him to
   a. not fuck your twin sister
   b. find your g-spot and a-spot[7]
   c. sit down when taking a piss
   d. None of the above. Instead you receive a blow to the head for having used the word "train" in regards to a human relationship.

8. What sorts of things does he do and say?
   a. "I have no interest in tying the knot with you, scagg."[8]
   b. "My married friends are such losers!"[9]

---

6 Marry him; probably not gay. (Disclaimer: Remember Oscar de la Hoya? Can not confirm non-gayness; we're all a little gay on the inside.)
7 HA! I bet you didn't know about the a-spot. (a-spot definition: another invention to make you feel inadequate even while you are coming.)
8 You should try harder. Maybe have a martini and his paper ready when he gets home. Pretty yourself up a little–no one wants to marry an ugo. Really!
9 Try harder. Just keep taking him out with Kate and Eric, and Vicki and Mark, and Jen and Daniel. Eventually he'll succumb to couple-dom. Trust me. Guys love to be coerced.

    c. He's an accountant with the urge to merge. How you know: he spends more time with you than the boys—if any boys ever hung out with him in the first place. After all, he did choose to be an accountant.
    d. He continually makes you cry.[10]

9. Sex happens
    a. every night
    b. when he's drunk and can stand the sight of you
    c. every Tuesday after dinner at your parents' and after you have folded all the laundry for the week and never outside of this allotted time, which he sweetly refers to as, "the scheduled Tuesday meeting of [y]our bodies"
    d. he won't touch you[11]

10. You are both between the ages of
    a. 10 and 15[12]
    b. 16-19
    c. 20-29
    d. 30+[13]

---

[10] Lucky girl. You're sharing feelings.
[11] Oh-oh! You must have done something to deserve that.
[12] It's not wrong. You're just like Mary in the bible (Can anyone say shameful teenage pregnancy?) or Romeo and Juliet in Shakespeare; your love transcends time and legal, moral, and decent boundaries.
[13] Seriously now. Jesus died when he was 33. Who wants to marry someone who is almost dead? Uhhh. No one! Do you even have any estrogen left in your body!?!

Let's tally your score:

1. a-0, b-0, c-10,000, d-0
2. a-0, b-0, c-1, d-0
3. a-0, b-0, c-is the right answer for all of the questions everything else would result in a wrong marriage, d-0
4. a-0, b-0, c-give him my number, d-0
5. a-0, b-0, c-please, 12, d-0
6. a-0, b-0, c-I'm a wedding planner, d-0
7. a-0, b-0, c-You'll know how serious he is if he calls me, d-0
8. a-0, b-0, c-I'm also a couples counselor–if you feel like he needs some persuasion, d-0
9. c-Just give him my number bitch!
10. c-All I want is a little bling. Is that so wrong? I'm over thirty; I ALREADY FEEL THE SAHARA IN MY WOMB. Please! Please put me out of my misery. For the love of God![14]

---

14 So you'll give him my number, right?

TELL ME.
WHY DOES HE HAVE TO HAVE A HEAD?

This all started when Niall grilled me about which athletes have the best bodies.

"Fucking fighters," he said.

And contemplating his decorated amateur boxer bod and the many times he had flexed his bodacious biceps for me, I agreed. Niall is ridiculously hot. Hotter still when I imagine him in silky shorts, topless, sweating and beating blood outta someone like a brutal poet of hurt.

Since grade four when I first watched *Gandhi* the movie, I loved Gandhi the man. He just had a way about him–this ability to conquer his tyrannical equestrian English overlords with the powers of his heart and mind. Sweet Gandhi: prophetic peaceful and awe inspiring. However, how-eh-ver... if Gandhi were my boyfriend and we were at a coffee shop and he were holding my hand and whispering in my ear about the zenish merits of turning the other cheek, when along came a winking Oscar de la Hoya–a de la Hoya who asked me to meet him in the washroom downstairs just so he could touch my pussy a little–I'd break Mahatma Gandhi's heart in a snap over my knee like a bamboo peace-pipe. And then dash to the washroom my mouth eagerly salivating–well c'mon! I'd wanna suck Oscar's cock a little too: he's de la Hoya. Have you seen that man? Ha-ot!

My desire for a fighting man downstairs and a thinking man upstairs made me ponder shit. Yes shit. About all the shit I had doled out to my boyfriends. The harder I pushed Noah away, the more I turned him down in bed, the more I complained about his music, the way he dressed, his porn, the more I got. I got a violin, a trip to the Bahamas, my weight in magic mushrooms. I didn't even have to keep myself fit or anything. I just had to bitch and moan and I got. And Noah isn't alone. There's Jake, and Kyle, Nelson and Sam, Brian and Richard, and Tom. Common thread: shit and love. The more shit I doled out the more love I got back. I hurt and I hurt and I hurt some more and in return I got essays written for me, free booze, sex when *I* wanted it, clothing, concert tickets, a snowboard, and a most invigorating ego-boost. Ah! There's nothing like unconditional love. As long as you're not the poor sap in love.

And then I fell in love. But that wasn't enough.

He fell out of love. And I was hurt. The kinda love-hurt that transforms you into a waste case.

Today, I am the nice girl. I'm also a very single girl—a very single girl expert in the art of self-love with a broken vibrator and an injured index finger. I can't hurt a soul.

So when Niall tells me I should take up boxing, I think maybe a hard bod and hitting are not such bad ideas.

I decide to model myself after Oscar de la Hoya, Oscar de la Hoya and Niall.

When Niall says, "You should go to Atlas to learn how to box," I go to Atlas. And when Niall says, "Those fucking gloves you are using are toxic pieces of shit," I take his advice and buy a train ticket to Montreal to get some Rival bag gloves. And when he asks, "What the fuck does everyone find so fucking funny about shoveling Kian's roof to spar?" I laugh. Mistake.

I am shoveling Kian's roof, right now... while they watch. Niall–Niall is telling Kian a lot of stories that involve the word fuck.

Fuck he's doing it in a sexy way.

Tell me. What could be wrong with wanting a piece of that?

There, on the roof, my blue toque on, my deltoids twitching and me, doing my best boy impression taking breaks to talk about surfing porn on Xtube and smoke cigars, they start talking about the past.

Kian says, "Niall. School is BS anyway. The most useful thing I ever learnt was when my gym coach told me sex was like basketball: You always dribble before you shoot."

Niall laughs hard and loud and feels better about when he dropped out.

He says, "Yeah. But I don't fucking know. Lately everyone around me seems so fucking stupid that I think I'm smart. Like I'm smarter than everyone."

I pipe up, "Well you are. You are. You could have done university like me easy. I just don't think you would have liked it because it's full of wankers. There are stupid people everywhere. But, you're intelligent. I think you are one of the most intelligent people I know."

And it's true, I do.

There was this one time when he drove me home. We were just sitting in front of my place talking and you expect him just to be this dumb mook ex-boxer guy but he said, "Karma! If one more fucking person says to me it's my fucking karma like that's a good fucking system to go on, I'm gonna hammer them straight in the fucking head. What the fuck is that? Karma! It's from one of the most oppressive fucking fucked systems—what's it called?—caste system. Fuck karma."

I'm not totally with him, but still if you take away all the fucks it's a pretty enlightened opinion, I think.

And I don't mind telling him so today.

"Well... I mean.... Fuck!" he turns away and fiddles with my shovel. "I wasn't trying to get you to say that I was smart or anything." And he's kinda blushing. And I think, wow, I just made this really tough guy blush. Like I have the upper hand.

That's about all of the softness that Niall can handle. He jerks Kian's shoulder, "We got a place to fight now. Get in there man!"

Kian takes off his jacket and under his tight shirt all is sinew—a bigger version of me. Kian gets into our make-shift ring.

Niall doesn't look at me. But I look at him.

I'm going to get my ass handed to me for breakfast, lunch, and dinner.

Niall shouts at me from the sides: "Get in your stance! What are you doing later anyway?"

Kian's circling me.

"I'm going to a cougar and cheese party," I say and throw out a jab that Kian catches too easy.

"I'm a fucking cougar."

"You're not a cougar, Niall. You can't be."

"Yeah I'm a cougar. I am. Me and Kian are coming."

And then he does this thing I hate. He gets my attention by waving and sticks out his chin and closes his eyes. Like I couldn't even hit him if I tried. And he calls me, "Boxing sweet-heart darling baby, baby baby baby."

I try to hit Kian so hard and he slips the punch.

I hate Niall.

But I want to make-out with him so bad.

I want him to touch me the way he used to.

It first happened when I got back from Montreal. I was bummed. Bummed by the girls that I know. Don't get me wrong, they make good friends, I just would never let any guy I know date one of them.

Marla was born to cheat. It's all she does—with every boyfriend. And now her husband. These poor guys, they never know. But the worst is when her and Sheila get together and try to teach Rory and I how to cheat.

"One. You never document it." This is what Sheila and Marla say to a tearful Rory who's just been caught. He read her diary.

I think, "Who keeps a diary at this age?"

Marla goes on and on about some masseuse she met at a bar, about the etiquette of who pays for the hotel room, about when to break it off. Sheila nods and opens another bottle of Shiraz.

But the best is when Marla and Sheila look at me and Roar and say, "Men deserve it. They're scum."

And just then the perfect masque of middle-class marriage begins. Colin comes in with Attie asleep on his shoulder. Marla kisses him and tells him to get a glass of wine while she takes Attie to bed. We all chit-chat: "Colin how was the dinner? Was Attie good? Oh my goodness! Did she really try to bite their little boy? How terrible. Poor little guy. Is he okay?"

I wish someone would punch me in the face.

When I Facebook all of this to Niall he's with me. He's just as sad and disgusted as I am, and even understands at the same times and in the same ways that I do.

He starts to tell me about his girl. About how she wants him to get a job and how she rags on him for never finishing anything he starts. She even brings up getting an education. Anyone who knows anything about Niall knows that's just not fair.

"You know I think you're awesome," I write.

"Yeah. Well I think you're fucking hot."

I take the opportunity to express my undying love, "So we'll anal when I get back?"

The message on Facebook when I finally get home: "You filthy filthy girl."

I blush.

And then every time I see him he touches me. Touches my knee. Touches the back of my neck. Whispers things in my ear. Once when I was standing at his kitchen sink he came up behind me and cupped his hand on my ass and then ran his other hand up my inner thigh. I almost cried it felt so good—so soft it stung. I can still feel it.

But today that's not what I get. I get Kian chopping down trees. Uppercut, left hook. Uppercut, left hook. Until my head is ringing and I warble, "Could someone please... pick up the phone?"

As Kian picks me up off my knees and Niall yells in my bleeding face, "Don't you fucking take a knee on me bitch. Get up! Get up!" I think of De la Hoya.

I think of the photos I saw of de la Hoya in drag.

I tell Niall as Kian lays me back in the snow to see how bad my lip is bleeding.

"Whatever. Have you seen de la Hoya's wife? Who the fuck cares if that guy wants to wear fishnets and wigs? He has balls big enough to do that shit. What the fuck are you watching that shit for? Leave de la Hoya to me. You should be watching Jorge Arse who hits to hurt. He's little, fast, precise. Fucking technique is what you need at your size to get you ready for your fight. Besides, he sucks a lollipop before a fight—he's a fucking girl." He chuckles and rubs my head like I'm his little brother.

This is how it's been since he got things back on track with his girl. She said she just wants him—wants him 'cause he's good enough the way he is. Like he'll do. I would treat him better than that.

I'm glad Kian's there at the cougar party. All the cats are all over Niall. He loves it. He's on a high. It's driving me crazy.

He's telling some story about beating some guy up because he looked at his girl the wrong way. I've heard it a million times.

The first time was on one of our Sunday night drives that were more about parking and talking than going anywhere. He told me he just doesn't like anyone messing with him when he's with his girl. So he's always ready.

"I think it's fucked that no one has ever done that for you. It's just like what a guy does. Protect his woman."

"I like to protect my girl." He reiterates for the ladies.

The gaggle is enthralled. I touch my lip and press on the part that's sore. My eyes well.

I blurt out, "I had the wickedest masturbation fantasy last night. I used this guy Marco Hill. He's so hot. You guys wanna see him?"

All the girls are in.

I don't look at Niall. But I can feel him. He's too quiet.

One of the girls asks, "What's he look like?" as I am scrolling through Niall's Facebook friends to find Mr. Hill.

"I don't know. You can't see his face. He's Muay Thai. Fucking hot."

"You had a fantasy about a guy and you don't know what he looks like!?!" one chick chirps.

"Believe me. The kinda hurt this guy was putting on me in the shower and the body he has.... I don't need his head."

When I get to the picture, all the girls have a look.

"It's just, like, a thumbnail photo."

I know something they don't and Niall knows I know it too.

"What? You're telling me you've never whacked off to a miniature picture before? Look at the guy's legs, his stomach... it hurts my pussy just to look at his body."

Kian mouths, "I've yanked to little pics."

I laugh out loud and look at Niall. He's staring hard.

The girls get bored faster than I did of Niall's story. They go back to the kitchen—go back to their wine. Kian follows.

I feel tight, on the mark and powerful.

This is what heads are for: to knock someone out doesn't take a lot of force; you just need to jostle the brains a little.

Niall looks like he's suffering from whiplash. He's studying me, all the vaingloriousness of earlier shaken right out of him.

I knew this when I started: Niall still pretends that back in high school his girl wasn't fucking his best friend—they both pretend. They pretend she still doesn't like Marco Hill better.

Niall gets up and struts over to me with a smirk on his face.

"That was pretty fucking sharp, bitch. Pretty quick. Must be your fight night; you got me right here fucker."

He taps his chin.

He's face to face with me, looking at me like he's beaming proud of me.

I'm grinning from ear to ear. I got him, got him like only a bitch could.

And I can finally feel it. I'm going to get what I want—what I want so badly from Niall: his special touch.

And it starts with his hand on my chest lightly and it's over before I even see it coming; he's that fast when he hits me square on the jaw.

And it's that hard that it sends my head snapping back.

And I fall.

And I see lines and iridescent blobs, and then black.

The pain is so deep it knocks a thousands hurts I've given and got right out of me.

And I love this hurt.

I love this hurt because it is not just in my head, it is real and it binds us. Out of the dark Niall's hand is a burst of white light like a lotus opening and I reach up to take it. From the black liquid vacuum Niall pulls me to him long through a straw.

I feel different. Cleansed. Stretched. Strong. Open. And love.

And when Niall's not looking, I laugh something secret: Praise be Oscar for pain, yes. But also, Thank Gandhi for Karma.

HOW AN INTERNET QUIZ SAVED MY LOVE-LIFE AND MADE ME SOME MONEY TOO

Are you dating a man, a myth or an animal?

One of the reasons it's so hard to tell if you are dating a man is that they are always changing. Am I right, or am I right ladies?

I am right.

Here is a quiz-taker's testament:

I was so confused. One minute he'd be there and then I'd look away and he was gone. And when we were out with one of my girl friends, I'd suddenly find out he had an interest in Gregorian chant if she said she was doing medieval studies, or a fine appreciation of Riesling wines if she ordered white wine. Was I dating a stranger, a renaissance man or a total bastard? I was *wowed*! by this insightful quiz. It's so true; I'm just with a wild legendary creature. Now our relationship is magical and I understand him so much more in the bedroom too!

Answer these questions honestly and we'll tally your answers to let you know how much man, animal-man or myth-man your man is.

1. If you are at a wine and cheese and you ask your lover to get you a refill
   a. he goes to the bar and comes right back with a full glass

b. he disappears into the crowd and you don't see him again for the rest of the night until you go to get your coat and he emerges from the on-suite bathroom from a cloud of mist looking all dewy happy but saying he was sick the whole night
   c. he goes to the bar and comes back empty handed because he says nobody at the bar noticed him but you could have sworn he was talking to a leggy blond
   d. he goes nowhere. You've got legs. Bitch, get your own drink!

2. What colour are his eyes?
   a. brown (Boring! But trustworthy.)
   b. blue (Get out now! LOL. Seriously though, can you trust anyone with blue eyes?)
   c. green (He's smarter than you. I just thought you should know.)
   d. hazel (Is that even really a colour? Or is it just something brown-eyed people tell themselves to feel special?)

3. When you point out that your biological clock is ticking, does he
   a. check his bank statement and then tell you his clock hasn't made a peep
   b. ask if you really think you will make a fit mother
   c. panic and fade into the background
   d. ask your best friend (who is so much more interesting than you) out to talk it over

4. How did he first ask you out?
   a. approach you outside of a high school dance and tell you there was a pot of gold in his pants[1]
   b. did it come out of nowhere[2]
   c. did you ask him out[3]
   d. did he just impress you so much with the extreme powers of his long long tongue[4]

5. Does he look like
   a. Johnny Depp
   b. Will Smith[5]
   c. Matthew McConnaughey
   d. or this

---

[1] Yes: most common answer for girls 12 and under (works almost as well as candy. Mmmm can anyone say: time for gold-wrapped chocolate-cock?).
[2] Like seriously, even now, does cum keep shooting at you from out of nowhere?
[3] Sorry! It was over before it even started.
[4] Hang onto him for dear life.
[5] Now that he is in this quiz, he is no longer just a token in Hollywood. Way to go Will!

If you answered mostly a, keep him! Oooo, your man's a little leprechaun! Exotic![6] You may have noticed that he has a way of confusing you with tales, cunning and his obsession with buckles. Has he? He may be the type to ride and run but he's worth it even if you're not!

If you answered mostly b, he's wild, he's crazy. He's crazy-wild. Like a chameleon.[7] He'll probably disappear by pulling a coyote morning.[8] This one's a catch! Don't let go... if you can find him.

If you answered mostly c and d, you are with a true leprechaun-chameleon man, he will do everything wrong. He'll cheat. He'll lie. He'll talk down to you. He'll never help with household chores. But he really does have a pot of gold! And even when he marries you, and you have kids with him, and you have a nice house, a Beemer, and a totally gratuitous SUV Porsche–i.e., a life together–he'll still let you use the credit card and, every once in a while, he'll even leave a little cash bonus on the nightstand before he does what he calls his walk of shame to work. He's so cute! Hang onto him.

If you answered a mix of a, b, c, and d but conclusively answered d on question five, you're with just a man.[9] Good luck! Hang on in there!

---

6 Exotic like Lucky Charms.
7 Oh those madcap chameleons!
8 You wake at dawn to his howls in the distance and find his dismembered arm under you. What an ANIMAL! You, you're a failed beaver trap.
9 Let's face it, you probably don't deserve any better.

WARNING: ALL CHARACTERS AND EVENTS IN THE FOLLOWING STORY—EVEN THOSE BASED ON REAL PEOPLE—ARE COMPLETELY AUTHENTIC. DUE TO ITS CONTENT, THIS STORY SHOULD NOT BE VIEWED BY ANYONE THAT I KNOW.

THIS STORY IS WEARING A LABCOAT: VERY SCIENTIFIC!

Before we begin, let's revisit grade nine science.

How to perform an experiment:

1. Define the question

2. Gather information and resources (observe)

3. Form hypothesis

4. Perform experiment and collect data (materials)

5. Analyze data

6. Interpret data and draw conclusions that serve as a starting point for new hypothesis

7. Publish results

8. Retest (frequently done by other scientists)

PROBLEM

"There was the time after drinking a few beers and walking on the DVP, I jumped on this guy Jeff and started making out with him. *He* said no."

I feel I've made my point.

Me 1. Paul 0.

I figure Paul doesn't need to know about THE PHOTO. The photo that Gintz enlarged and hung over his bed. The photo of me smiling a big big dumb smile, squatting–a huge puddle of steaming urine creeping around the side of me, my hand smack dab, leaving my sleeve urine soaked. Jeff took the photo. So maybe it's not so strange that he said no. Go figure, urine just doesn't make some guys hot.

"There is no way a guy would say no," says Paul.

Me, Paul, 0 all.

"But I am telling you man: every guy says no," I say.

"There was Mike: he said no. And Si and Ty: they said no. And...."

"Yeah. Fine. But was it a cold-call come-on?"

"No."

"Well that doesn't count. None of it counts. I'm saying that if you ask a guy on the street, he will not be able to refuse."

"And I'm saying there is no way that would work. There are too many factors."

"Factors!?! I'd go home with any decent girl that asked me."

He wouldn't.

Would he?

Would any man?

OBSERVATIONS

THE BENCHMARKS OF MASCULINITY:

Just like Sam on *Cheers* or Dan on *Night Court* there is some girl out there whose stupefying boobs are overshadowed only by her fabulously teased and permed hair, willing, wanting, waiting for you to say yes, yes to her request to have nameless sex in the janitor's supply closet.

Off stage is the place to be a man: fucking is what matters. How many broom closets have you received hand-jobs in? Did you bend her over the pail and plunge her head into its grey water? Did you take perfect aim and mark your glory in a spunky stain on her cheap satin blouse?

Chicks who never just took it: Diane, Miss Howe, and Christine.

Those ladies may have been love interests but could never slut it up enough to turn the male stars into real men via a good broom-closet banging.

When I was eight watching *Mash*, I decided that I want to help guys–help guys become men. I want to take their pale doughy boy bodies and turn them into hard and brilliant as jade Hawkeyes. Like Florence Nightingale–but a pretty one–I too will hold a torch, or many, through the night.

HYPOTHESIS

TV is bad for eight year-old girls?

Florence Nightingale was a ho?

TV men get nasty-laid; Toronto men do not?

PAUL DECIDES: One, a female one, could get laid just by asking.

EXPERIMENT

Making an experiment can be very difficult. How many people need to be asked? Are there types of questions that could change the result in unforseen ways?

"To do this thing right," I say to Paul, "we need to try to make every part of the experiment the same, except for the thing we want to test."

Pauls says, "It's called a variable."

"Yeah. Thanks Paul. I know."

Our variable: the guy.

PAUL'S STIPULATIONS AND LIMITATIONS: I must be sober enough to seem attractive. I must never use the word fuck directly. The word fuck would scare target. (For fuck's sake!) I must always ask within one half-hour of primary contact. Otherwise there may be emotions.

"Dude! I'm willing to admit that some lonely asshole might say yes to coming home with me... maybe... but there is no guy *alive* who falls in a half hour."

Paul kindly reminds me that that is a different experiment.

Thanks for keeping me on track Paul.

DIAGRAM 1
THE TRACK

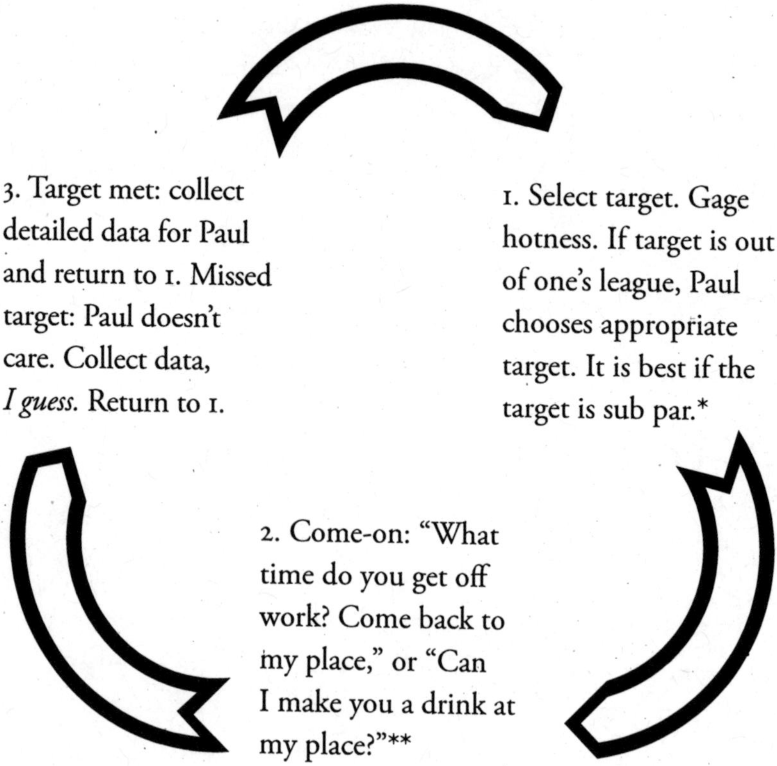

1. Select target. Gage hotness. If target is out of one's league, Paul chooses appropriate target. It is best if the target is sub par.*

2. Come-on: "What time do you get off work? Come back to my place," or "Can I make you a drink at my place?"**

3. Target met: collect detailed data for Paul and return to 1. Missed target: Paul doesn't care. Collect data, *I guess*. Return to 1.

*Paul's really looking out for me on this one.

**My rejected suggestions: "When do you get off? When I tell you you can, all over my face," or "Can I make you a drink by riding my snail-trail[1] from your cock over the roughage of your chest hairs straight up to your mouth?"[2]

---

[1] Sadly, at no time can I scream, "Stroke the snail. Stroke my slimy snail!" in reference to petting my pussy. Paul's so uptight.
[2] Uh! Mmmm. Savor the flavor of escargot.

To secure the identities of all targets they shall be referred to hereafter as Dave or some Dave variable.

MATERIALS

1. Silly drink order with high mess and spill potential: tester may lick sticky substances from her own various body parts... at any time.

2. Gum.

3. Perfume.

4. A low-cut top.

5. And a thirst for knowledge.

FIRST TARGET: Former-Drummer Dave.

This Dave once worked with Paul. Paul assures me that he is the perfect Dave. This Dave is soft: recently single; due for a rebound. I agree to this Dave: He's got nice forearms. And, I'm due for a single rhythmic kit work-over.

Issue: Little mutual Paul-me trust. I think Paul will prime or pressure the Dave explicitly or implicitly into submission. Paul thinks I'll botch the job intentionally.

"But I'm seriously intent on making-out. I swear!"

He isn't having it.

Enter third party: Norm–unbiased observer.

Norm keeps time. I have twenty-nine minutes and counting. I approach the bar. "Dave, you get off at two right? You should come over to my place after." Facial response: shock. Answer: "I'll let you know." Confer with Paul and Norm. When Dave will not approach our table for the next two hours we all agree: Dave's a no-go.

OTHER NOTABLE DAVES:

Dave rubber-necker: Couldn't keep his eyes off any girl in the place. Who was he saying yes to!?! Paul decides it doesn't matter: any yes is a yes. I disagree. Final vote: Yes via Paul veto.

German-Dave looked very excited: came at my proposal–like actually cum in his pants. Paul and Norm called it premature. I just call it efficient. Unanimous yes vote.

END DATE: after 50 guys

"Paul! What are you insane? The intern at my last gyno visit dropped her jaw when I revealed my count. I can't potentially add even a third of fifty new dudes to the list. They'll start asking me what I take in tax-free dollars per head, or head given, or head endured…."

Paul says, "Just think of the apes."

"What the–are you talking about?"

"Think of Jane Goodall. We all have our brunt to bear for science."

When Paul's right he's right.

But still, an ape analogy. What is Paul thinking about?

DATA/ANALYSIS

"Screw D and A!" Paul said.

And certainly if you added two more letters, that would pretty much sum up my approach to this section: screw Dave on my back, on my side, in my lap, or from no-Dave to little Daves all over my face and in my crack.

There were many, many many no's but I try not to think about that. I try not to think about it while Paul retells those stories at friends' barbeques. Anyway....

That's the very abridged version.

On to the scientific money shot:

CONCLUSION

"Norm. Paul. That's been the hardest earned and best got gonorrhea of my life."

"Dude! No worries. That's so treatable. And just think. You get to say I was wrong and you were right—with a report—guys really do say no to you."

Thanks again Paul. Thanks.

APPENDIX: AFTER THE FACTS

We tried really hard to publish our results. But nothing really got done until Paul started dating a blond scientist. I know! I was surprised too: scientists do come in blond. And she's a real scientist!

Mostly she told us that our experiment wasn't real science.

So she took us all to Madagascar to be her field assistants.

Paul, Norm and I really didn't learn a lot about science, I don't think. But we did learn a lot about touching and sorting lemur poop.

When Paul couldn't take it anymore he left and took the real scientist with him.

I continued to catalogue poop... for no reason. I catalogued the poop and told Norm everything I know. Not about poop, but about Dave.

When I strutted to the bar to talk to Dave, another man approached me to take my drink order. I leaned on bar, ass in air in a Paulapproved pose. I ordered my drinks. Dave took one look at my presenting ass and said, "I've got this one." And did he ever!

Former-drummer Dave was no no. He was a yes and what a yes he was.

Here's what he really said: "I can't wait 'til after work. Meet me upstairs and I'll fuck your tight little box so hard."

When I went back to the table, that was not a look of disappointment on my face but a look of bewilderment: I had no idea my legs could bend that far behind my head; I had no idea that four fingers could fit in my tiny virgin anus; and I had no idea how filthy a real broom closet is.

Norm thinks this makes a pretty good story.

When we get back he's going to publish an extended version of it called *These Are The Daves She Knows*. You know, to appeal to the *Kids In The Hall* generation.

I tell him I want to publish our findings somewhere.

When Norm went back and told Paul, Paul thought that was a pretty quaint idea. He said, "What a quaint non-scientific little head she has."

Thanks. Paul.

Norm tells me Paul and science-girl got hitched. She got him a job at Johns Hopkins and now Paul feels all high and mighty. I also heard about the separation.

Well I think it's time for a re-test. Only with different rules.

I sent Paul a letter from Costa-Rica detailing everything: the method.

I think he will be happy to know that things are going really well down here. Way better than they did with Toronto guys.

I came down here to Costa-Rica with his wife to learn more about science.

We have a quaint experiment we like to play every night called who gets to wear the pants. Sometimes it's her. Sometimes it's me. But she always lets me wear the labcoat.

We're having a gay old time!

I finally get the ape thing: primatologists are hot!

Wherever you are Paul, I just want you to know, your ex-wife is fucking me just great.

And I feel I've made my point: Paul 0, Me 1 billion trillion thousand six hundred and one… plus one.

Thanks Paul. No seriously. This time, really, thanks.

HOW TO DATE A GAY MAN

(I've dated so many.)

1. MAKING CONTACT: Try my two favorite pick-ups: "I don't care what anyone says. I like Paris. As in, Hilton. As if, there's any other." Or if you're type is a little more highbrow, try, "Oh my God! Toasted almond is my favorite drink too."

2. TAKE STOCK: Literally. Know which clothes are yours. Staple an inventory to the inside of your closet and visit it regularly. I warn you harshly; if you do not heed my advice you will look out the window one early morning and see a Uhaul speeding away with pieces of ball gowns trailing behind it and the odd Missoni shoe left in its wake. Face it. If he's not going to wear them (and oh he'll try) he'll give them to his girly-girl fruit flies. That's right. You'll be gownless and shoeless and see some young gay-lovin' ingenue (the kind you once were) wearing your duds saddling up to a tall kerchiefed blond man in a martini-bar. Single tear. Inventory! (Keep track of your shampoos too. The gays love to smell good.)

3. LAWS OF ATTRACTION: Stay open. Very open. So he may never fulfill your life-long dream of being finger-banged in an alleyway. And sure it may all be untousled Egyptian cotton sheets, but if you're open, you can have a little fun. Remember that Sigma Alpha Epsilon boy from second year—well you probably don't because you were drunk off jello shooters and playing in the basement raper-room—but he remembers you, and the good times. Have him over for dinner. Let your lady-boy cook up something deliciously

gourmet and unpronounceable and pretty soon they'll be male-bonding–male-bonding all over your body. Why use your body? It's the laws of attraction. They need an excuse to touch each other and the slab of uncooked chicken meat between your legs is the perfect conduit for male-on-male desire. Hey! You wanna get touched don't you!?!

4. JUST FOR FUN: Dress him up in your clothes. Literally–put the clothes on him and take them off him. I did this once with great results. First I set a bet: "There is no way you can fit into my skirt." But remember, he's gay: he's been watching his waist-line, you know he'll slip into everything you own but add disbelief to fan his already ferocious flaming flames: "Well you fit into that one but there's elastic in the waist, there is no way you'll fit into this pencil skirt" and so on. Very important: let your hands linger on his puerile hairless body as you button, unbutton, zip, and unzip while kneeling before him. A fun fact about the body: it has no control over arousal. You may actually get to fellate him. If it doesn't work, have the girls over, get them drunk on crantinis and listen to them gripe about sex as a chore and how much they hate sucking cock. *Yay*!

6. GETTING OUT: there is no out. Let's face it; the closet is a warm and cozy place. Would you come out of it? He won't. You can do whatever you like: sleep with other men, women, whatever. It won't work. 'Cause he's doing exactly what he likes–fucking anonymous men in movie houses, train station bathroom stalls and alleyways[1] and you are his alibi. He can run for office, get on the board, or

---

[1] Remember that finger-bang alley of your dreams? It's someone else's reality and his name is probably Reuben: *Gay*!

simply work for the CBC[2] and there relish a tawdry cornucopia of ass behind closed doors. Of course, as suggested in tip two, they do flee. But why? Well, for this I can use my most reliable point of gay married reference, *Far From Heaven*. Sure it's set in the fifties. But how much has really changed? According to the movie you need to take a vacation in a place where your boyfriend or husband has ass-access and lots of it. I'm thinking somewhere warm. Florida. Seriously. Think pink flamingos. Think sun, fun and speedos. Take a trip down. He's bound to go down on someone. Trust me. According to the movie, there he'll find his true love and finally spurn and leave you. It's, like, far from heaven but it may be your only way out. Fun!

---

[2] Canada's Biggest Closet.

DYLAN BEGEE HATED MY VIBRATOR

Dylan suffered from a floppy member. He was as flaccid as a piece of thread. Sometimes. The first time I dated him.

Okay. I meet Dylan in a wallow of post-break-up snot. Between dry heaves and gloppy mucous wails he feeds me kamikaze shots with Jagger chasers. He swears to take good care of me for the night.

And I... am eager to put myself in able hands.

Now we're drunk. Really drunk. So.... I can't remember the details. But I'm pretty content when I wake up buck, beside a sweet naked soccer ass. Content, satisfied, proud–I got a tight little lay. Yep. I'm a super-star. Over one boy and under the next. I... basically... ROCK THE COCK.

That's right. I do.

I do in my head 'til Dylan says, "It was the booze. Sorry."

Now, that's alright. I mean. It happens? Right? I'm okay with it. "I'm okay with it," I say.

We date. Months pass. Dylan makes dinner. I rent movies. We laugh. We're a couple. A happy couple.

155

First, he blames it on nerves. Then on inexperience. And then, finally, on a rare psychological disorder that "I swear I'm trying to fix with my therapist. I swear."

I figure: a) I have a mutt face. b) Am too much of a slut to deserve real love and/or c) Dylan is as queer as a rainbow cucumber.

Now, I'm not being entirely fair. Dylan did, every once and a while, get his Rip Van Winkle to rise.

Once, after snorting coke off my inner thigh, he really got off. He put his hands behind his head and fucked me like a rock-star!

A clammy, coked-out, middle-aged rock-star.

I had to do something.

I decided to finish myself off in the shower. But when I slipped "big-pink" out from under my pillow, Dylan–high, satiated Dylan– looked at me and whined. He whined! Like a boxed alley-puppy in the rain.

I put my vibrator back under the pillow and rolled onto my side.

I know I'm making this sound bad. But really he's a nice guy and we laugh. He makes me laugh and the couple that laughs together stays together. So we're staying together.

I get him a summer job at a camp for the anglophone challenged. And this is okay. Us working together, works okay.

Until gender-ambiguous Jesse.

Dylan crosses the line. Dylan starts to fuck one of his flirts. And as if that's not bad enough, she has man-hands. You heard me. His new lady friend has the hands of a card-carrying chicken-choker. *That's* my competition.

For the rest of the time at camp I foster a well-developed complex about my less-than-feminine figure.

Does Dylan like his ladies to look like dudes? Is that why he was with me?

Well I don't want that. I want a normal guy. A guy who wants a girlfriend. A relationship. I want to cross into the realm of absolute straightdom. I want my long and winding road to turn into a direct A to B that ends at a white picket fence with a rose bush and a golden retriever in the yard.

I decide I'm too thin. So, I stop running, eat copious amounts of bacon and force myself to park it in front of *Friends* reruns for hours in the hopes of developing child-bearing hips. An under-wire fake foam boob-builder bra is a must. I don dresses twenty-four seven. And lipstick. My god lipstick! Why didn't anyone ever tell me I had my father's weak mouth? But with a little colour.... Presto! it looks like I have lips that could cushion a tail pipe. I'm a perfect lady.

And this stuff really works!

At the final dance, Travis, another teacher, catches me fixing my up-do in one of the mirrors.

He laughs.

He thinks I'm vain.

I've been caught being vain and faking girl and trying too hard and he knows it, so he laughs. I turn around fast. And I'm a little red. "Hey," he snorts. I try to walk away. He holds my arm. "That's a nice pink dress, hot stuff." He whispers this in my ear: "Wanna dance?"

A half an hour later, his hand finds its way to my ass.

I can't help myself. I've been prepping for this moment. I haven't had sex for a month. I've been thinking about sex for a month. And Travis is different. Travis is flirtatious. Travis is new and cute. And... something else.... I can't quite put my finger on it. Oh yeah. Travis is hard!

Thank God!

In fact, that's what I do most of the night: "Oh God Yes! Sweet Jesus that tongue, that t-t-t-ongue... uh, oh... right.... GOD! Please. Ungh. Please!.... Get on our knees. Oh. Oh! OH! GOD!" and so on.

In the morning, I go to grab my dress off his bed and see, at the foot of his bed, him. A picture of him. A picture of Travis kissing–full on the lips crazy hardcore kissing–a man.

I am soooo naked right now.

I hear Travis turn over.

I hold my dress up to try to cover myself.

"Hey," he says. He says, "Good Morning."

I am staring at the picture.

He points. "Oh." He points and he says, "That's me and J at five years."

"Come here. I wanna spoon ya," he says.

Spoon me! Fuck you!

But I don't say this. Instead, I start to cry and rumple up on the floor like a sickbed snot-rag.

In this moment... okay, so you're gonna hate me for this but... I think about Dylan. I think about how *good* things were with him.

At least he made me really great omelettes with red pepper smiles and chive eyes.

Why can't I have him? Why can't I? Jesse has him and I don't? That he-bitch.

All that consoles me is that maybe Dylan still can't get it up.

And then it comes like a long-distance Christmas package of treats through the mail: sweet sweet relief.

"I'm sorry."

"Dylan?"

"Is Travis there?"

"That's not your business."

"You're right. I'm sorry," he says for the second time in two seconds.

"How's things with Jess?"

"We ended it. You know... end of the summer. We were coming home anyway."

"Listen," he says, "I wanted to talk to you. There are some things I had to say. I want.... Can we try to make us better?"

I hold back. "We'll see."

That night, Dylan shows up at my reading.

We're standing there with friends—two other couples we were cooped up with last Valentine's in a tiny cottage. Stu and Sarah are getting married this winter. Mike and Jenny broke up but got back together.

My turn.

Dylan pats me on the ass as I'm introduced. Things are definitely looking up.

ROUND TWO

We're walking home. Dylan left the bar with me and now we're strolling down St. Laurent in silence. A comfortable silence. Every once and a while he points to something in a storefront that I might like: a Mos Def record, a pink dress, a Canucks jersey (that one's as much for him as me).

He takes my hand in his.

I stiffen. "I don't know," I say. "Dylan I...."

"I love you."

What!?!

Okay. Wait.

He loves me!?!

He loves me.

I'm swooning. I actually am. I'm weak in the knees like a Southern belle standing on her daddy's big porch, the air fat with the smell of magnolias, about to say yes to her beau's marriage proposal. This is so lame... but it's true.

Dylan has my hand in his. We're standing below a streetlight. He takes my other hand. He looks me straight in the eye and says, "I think I love you."

Whoa. This is soooo hot.

At home, I ride him and his face into two orgasms.

Dylan's feeling like a champ. In a third attempt, he flips me onto my stomach, grabs my vibrator and goes in for the motorized reach-around.

He can't turn it on.

I chime, "Failed batteries?"

But he's determined to make a go of it. And he does. Manual style. That night, Dylan gives me the best digitally enhanced penetrative orgasm of my adult years.

Our troubles are officially over.

For a while.

Don't get me wrong. The sex, surprisingly, stays good. Surprisingly good. Yeah. A little too good. And I start to wonder. I wonder what happened to make things so different. And if he went from such a limpy-magee to a hard-hammer jack-rabbit... I mean... can he handle it?

I have this dream. I dream that Dylan is at a family reunion with me. There's this giant buffet and I can't find him. I race through hillocks of junky food: jell-o kebobs, mountains of bad Anglophone poutine with oodles of half-melted mozzarella peaks, plastic-covered-for-your-protection strawberry sundaes. Until, finally, I find Dylan sitting atop a massive pancake stack holding what looks like Christmas pudding in one hand and a chocolate metronome in the other. He looks almost regal. Then, in slow rotation, he takes a bite out of the pudding, then the metronome and then he bends over at the waist and takes a bite of pancake. And the pancake stack seems to grow higher and higher taking Dylan up, up and away... from me. I say something to him, but he can't hear me; he's too high up. I ask him about our plans Friday but he just goes on eating: the pudding, the metronome, the pancake. I can barely hear what I am asking through his loud mastication. And then, I see it. His hands are the Christmas pudding and the metronome. And he's eating his knees! And he really likes it! He looks really happy.

The next night, I tell Dylan the dream. One up: I tell him what I think it means.

"Maybe you're not satisfied... with me."

"But it was your dream," he says.

"I know. But... you know? I have to listen to what my dreams are telling me. And, I think, maybe I am not enough for you. I mean, with all those dripping cock symbols and you eating yourself and enjoying it so much, maybe you want a another kind of...."

"You are the only person who thought Jesse had man hands. For Christ's sake. Stop trying to make me gay."

Just then the bartender walks by and smirks.

Dylan looks down and mutters, "Jesus. I have to take a piss."

I order up two kamikaze shots and toss them back like lemonade. I'm working up to something but I'm not quite sure what.

When Dylan comes back form the washroom, I start up as if he had never left.

"What was it then? What changed? Viagra?"

"This isn't the place," he says.

I'm not listening.

"I mean. I changed. I changed the way I dress. The way I act. Is it that? 'Cause I would like it if it was me that helped you, you know, feel better. Or prefer it. Or something. I would prefer it if it was me and not her. I just want to know that we're riding the same track. That I'm enough for you the way you are enough for me?"

He takes a sip, "You're too complicated."

"What do you mean?" I want for this to come out defensive, like I don't know what he's talking about, but it comes out like I think it. Like I agree but want to know the kinds of complicated he means: the exact details of his interpretation of my brand of complicated.

"I don't know. Okay. It's just something I'm saying. Okay."

He just looks at me like he's tired.

"Fuck you," I say this into my drink.

"No," he says. He says, "Fuck you," straight to my face. "You're too demanding. Nothing's ever easy with you. Nothing."

He says, "I'm getting another drink."

He stops. "No. Hang on…" and smirks. "That's right. You're easy. Everything else about you is so fucking fucked up."

Wait.

It gets worse before it gets better.

Worse is Fiona.

I hear later that Dylan left the bar with and is now dating a seventeen-year-old virgin that we taught in the summer. Fiona's perfect. Fiona has wavy brown hair down to her ass. Fiona giggles at everything Dylan says. And Fiona's happy in the world. She's unblemished by the simple experiences of living on her own. She has never had to buy single-ply toilet paper so she can afford Monistat meds to relieve her feminine itch… which brings me back to Fiona's most perfect part: her unpenetrated poon. Fiona is the literalization of my fears. I'm nothing. Nothing but a skinny, face-sitting, doggy-styling, slut-face whore.

And for days I can't stop the hate train in my brain.

Maybe if I hadn't said fuck you. Maybe if I laughed more or talked less or maybe I have too many opinions. Why can't I keep my opinions to myself? I talk too much. I'm too out there. My clothes are loud. I should just back off. Too pushy. I'm too much for people. I expect too much from people. I'll grow my hair. I'll grow my hair and buy wrinkle cream.

Until, I can't take it anymore.

I decide to whack-off through the pain.

I find my vibrator where Dylan threw it: near the heater. My pretty pink pleasure engine has melted into the shape of a Smurf hat.

This is not what I need. But, I'm desperate.

I turn on the vibe and stare at it. It looks like Gargamel has put a manic nodding yes spell on a Smurf hat.

What would you do?

I'm too sad to laugh.

So I put the pink freak to work.

God love him. Dylan Begee finally fulfilled his purpose in my life. He had accidentally crafted me a g-spot cock-rocket.

At last, I was in the throws of lasting love and I only had to ask once: "Are we there yet, Papa Smurf?"

JARED: A PSYCHOLOGICAL PORTRAIT OF A SUBWAY DAUPHIN IN CD'S

Some people become famous through sheer determination and strength of character. Think Lance Armstrong. Think the miraculous unity of body and will. To become famous, Lance won the Tour de France seven times. If athletic genius exists, it's in Lance Armstrong. And, as if conquering grueling hills multiple times with legs like Peugeot pistons isn't enough, the guy went and beat testicular cancer. Now that, that is a hero.

Well to the hero Lance Armstrong I say, balls.

What is truly heroic is the battle against the bulge. Lance probably had it easy from the start: looks, leanness, the works. He was practically built for fame. But what I want to know about is accidental fame. I want to hear the story of the fat guy gone thin—it's the quintessential tale of will against body. Call me a self-flagellating guilt-ridden Catholic as much as you like, but if God had intended for us to be nice to ourselves, he would not have invented Dunkin' Donuts and then the Bowflex. And if ever there were a prince to represent fat-to-thin fame by accident, it's Jared. What an accident he was! He ate less and walked more and voila! Fame.

From my couch I say to Jared, "Good on you for making Lance Armstrong look like a dimwit try-hard."

Jared:

1. I think that when Jared started dropping the weight and appearing on television he probably picked up more than a few honeys. Because he wasn't used to all of the sexual attention and the ladies just wanting a piece of his lean meat, Jared had his heart broken more than a few times. Oh Jared. Just listen to these sage lyrics: *It could have been so beautiful, it could have been so right and she could have been your lover of every day of your life. But you don't want could have been on a cold and lonely night.* No doubt, Jared has a collection of sad-boy CD's. His favorite sad-boy CD? Surprise surprise: *Tiffany* featuring "Could've Been" by Tiffany. I'm sure he had it on repeat for days.

2. He is a "celeb." He needs a glam profile. He wants a little edge. (But he still tucks in his flannel shirts.) Where does a boy go in the pop-culture world to add a little bite to his fledgling nice-guy stardom? Gwen Stefani. That's right. Our boy Jared loves *The Sweet Escape*. (Actually, Jared's burnt; he's on the cutting room floor for "Wind it Up." The whole vid was his concept.)

3. Jared loves the air-drums. In fact, he formed an all-air-instruments band in college. To relive those garage glory days, the J-man heads to the shed, throws on G N' R "Use Your Illusion" (1998), and RAWKS OUT! He plays his drums, his old buddy Mike's ethereal base and does a back to back with Mike as Greg the ultimate air-guitarist. Oh! Those hands! That technique! All this happens under the delusion that he is building things for his fixer-upper home. Ah. Dreams.

4. Pearl Jam *Ten*—it's so obvious that Jared would own this CD. (See flannel shirts.)

5. My wild card: The Refused "The Shape of Punk to Come." If Jared does own this CD, there is something he is hiding from all of his burn-the-bulge, die-hard fans. Maybe he visits peep-shows in New York. Maybe Jared's suburban dream home is, in fact, a crack den. Maybe, it means he's gay. Or, worse, maybe Jared is actually... come to think of it, what's worse than being gay? Oh right, being gay Lance Armstrong. Or gay into bestiality Lance Armstrong. Or, well, to be honest, just being Lance Armstrong would suck.

HOW TO DATE A LAWN BOWLER

(I, am not ageist, just racist.)

1. LAWN BOWLING IS NOT SEXY. You are probably ahead of me on this one. I still haven't quite learnt the nuances of resisting the green. I've been "leaning over the fence" watching the balls since I was a fifteen year old Catholic schoolgirl. It's those, long bowling socks, pulled right up to the knee. And those white visors. Those flat shapeless shoes. Oooo. And I always loved untucking those whitey-white-white shirts and craved the feel of grey flannel on my teenage thighs. Ungh!

Is anyone else hot in here?

No?

Moving right along....

2. IT IS NOT BOCCE. You can't go around comparing lawn bowling to that dirty deigo version of the sport.[1] I mean, do you want to lose your lawn jockey lover? No. Then dear God stop calling it bocce. Lawn bowling is not bocce: a) because lawn bowlers are

---

[1] You're probably angry 'cause you're a wop or something, right? (Psss. It's okay. I can't be a racist; my mother's Italian. See, doesn't that comfort you? I know it's a comfort to me; I've been using her as a shield anytime I utter any anti-I-ty slander. I'm also a card carrying queer, I have a black friend and I joined a mosque. I'm a Swiss-guarded bigoted-comedy goldmine! Damn. Those Swiss are a silly people. I'm going to have to marry me a mountain-kraut.)

respectable looking senior citizens while bocce players are young grease-monkey Gino's; and b) bocce has music and looks fun. You don't want your lover having fun. It may disrupt his pace-maker.

Oh, excuse me. So you say that bocce is related to an ancient Roman game. So what? Next, are you going to get a shark, a lion and a Catholic and have them do the bloody butterfly in the kiddy pool in your backyard? Very Romanesque! Is that a "game" too?

3. AN IMPORTANT GOAL: Get used to the lingo. When your lawn-ball junky says, "I want to duck under the kitty," do not sit on his face. No no. The game is riveting but it's not as exciting as all that.

Actually we had better go over some terminology that could lead to great embarrassment on the green.[2] Close head, hand, the hammer, hammering the hole, and yard on, are not what they seem. Should you hear a phrase such as, "My vice has a yard on and is holding the shot bowl for the final hammer," it is not what you think.[3]

4. SWEET-TALKING YOUR BRAWNY BOWLER: So you don't know what it means to be a jack-bunny. It's okay. No one else does either. What's important is *how* you're a jack-bunny.

Tip 1: Be in the wheelchair know.

---

[2] Again, I would like to offer a formal apology to the Sister's of Mercy bowling club; I just didn't know what Sir Roland meant when he asked me to back wood his corridor of possibility.

[3] You have such a dirty mind. (I didn't think it! You did. God, you're dirty.) Can I give you my number?

Tip 2: Hospitals are the most fertile grounds for "free" wheelchairs.

Tip 3: After taking your golden age lover for a spin around his eight by four dormitory, saddle up, increase the volume on his hearing aid and whisper, "I'll be your legs daddy."

5. ENDING IT: Wait it out.

6. WHEW! Finally you've inherited everything and the balls. Now trade up. Take yourself to the salon for an acrylic nail refill, hairspray upside down, throw on that black mini-skirt and get your tail down to a bocce tournament.[4]

It's time for a slummin'-humpin'. *Yeehaw!*

---

[4] Those Ginos play on broken oyster shells–so exotic! (Oo. How I do love a good othering.)

CHUCK-CHIK

Chuck-Chik used to love to drink swamp mix. Down by the school after hours right out of a Mason jar. As the liquor levels went down at home and his dad's temper rose Chuck-Chik just shrugged: must be evaporation. That's the thing Chuck-Chik learnt in school. Otherwise, he studied Jenny Bandelli.

Jenny ran track right down by where Chuck-Chik drank. He watched her go round and round: she went the distance. The distance but never all the way. I watched him watch her while I swigged off his drink. Jenny gave blow-jobs to Chuck-Chik behind the school after training. He wore his Drakkar Noir. When he got back I was always half-way through the booze. The front of his pants covered in red clay dust. I'd ask him if JB had given him a BJ. He wouldn't say. So I just kept asking. Had she checked his microphone, hood sucked him, given him a hummer, or my personal favorite, brought out for only very special occasions, "Did you fuck her sweet face?"

Then he caved, "Yeah" and always in her defense, "Just a little though."

But I wanted more. I begged him for details. He said Jenny was good. But how? *How?* Was it depth. Was it rhythm? Was it really really wet and soft? Is that how she did it? I wanted to learn. Learn in theory before I put it into practice—what can I say?—my family, we're book people.

Jenny was no book person. But Chuck knew she wasn't easy either.

Jenny wouldn't fuck Chuck because she was hold'n out for football players, or at least a tennis guy.

But she wasn't always so stuck-up.

Jenny, Chuck-Chik, and me go way back to JK. Back to the time before sunblock. We'd swim in an orange dragon blow-up pool and then lie out on the sidewalks to tan. Back to when we had a secret club under Jenny's porch. We'd pick poison berries and mash them up into water and then tell that Geoff Greenough kid from down the street it was lemonade. When he wouldn't drink it I'd pull down his pants and Jenny and Chuck'd laugh hard. We go back to when Chuck-Chik's older brother pointed at him and screamed, "Chuck-Chik chokes on dick!" after Chuck-Chik had missed the penalty shot that would have got them into the finals.

Me and Jenny walked him home. He was crying. We swore we'd never call him Chuck-Chik again. I said, "I'm gonna call you just Charlie."

Jenny, she calls him Charles.

We all go back to when I bit Charlie so hard I made him bleed. Jenny's mom wouldn't let her hangout with us and then she just wasn't allowed to hang out with me. I'm not the right kind of people. Even now we only know each other through Charlie.

I wait in the back of the church for Charlie to sneak out of Saturday night service. I wait 'til I can see Charlie genuflect, his dad giving him the evil eye across the pews. But what's he gonna do—beat him right there in church? Charlie walks toward me. Some things are more important than God or a beating. Like Coffee Time.

When Charlie and me skip mass we go to Coffee Time to talk. We talk about Jenny.

I tell him, "I know your past so I can see your future."

He says I'm full of it until I say, "You're gonna marry Jenny." And then I've got his attention so I run with it. "Listen. I'm telling the truth. She's goin' nowhere else."

"Whatever, guy!" Charlie tosses his mess of black curls back, laughing.

"I'm serious."

Charlie's not buying it. He snorts at me sideways.

"What? All she does is run in circles that end at your dick."

Charlie likes this. He wants to know more.

"You'll work with politically correct fake and bake vanilla lattes. Not like the lucky Staten Island or Brooklyn I-ties working in Manhattan who get to work construction and smoke cigars and eat steaks with other I-ties. Naw. You'll never work in a place where you get to use the word fuck in meetings. You'll work some middle management job at a bank or something. Maybe you can even move your dad up from the bocce lawns down the street to the lawn-bowling greens. Can you say wah-awsp? Shit ya. Capital double-U A S P!"

I'm screaming but Charlie's just staring at the ground.

"I thought you could do better than that."

I normally tell him about Porches and Vegas and girls–loads of girls. But this time I want to tell him the truth, like this time is for real.

"But that is better right? Better than what our parents got. It's a load better than being a plumber or a housewife or whatever. A step up. Maybe you'll even get to wear a name tag at your cake job. Oh oh! Who's a lucky fucker? Who is? I think you are."

Charlie flips me the bird; he's happy again.

"Seriously it's good. You'll make your dad mad by having three girls and no boys or somethin'. And every Good Friday you guys'll go down to little Italy and watch the parade. You'll buy the girls their cotton candy and tell them to be quiet. And you'll watch as Jesus comes along lying on a white padded sedan and after you're sure he's passed, then you guys will all start to talk and you'll tell Jenny and the girls that some things are easier in death than life. That a white cushy sedan is way better than the crown of thorns and blood and sweat and dehydration of the real Stations of the Cross. And then you guys will stop and get brunch–maybe at Cucina's even 'cause you can afford it on that big bank job, Daddy Warbucks."

I slush the sugar around in the bottom of my coffee cup.

"You'll make Jenny happy."

We get up, pay the old lady at the cash and start to walk. We're walking to the school. Charlie knows Jenny's training. We sit right in the middle of the field so she can see Charlie.

"What about you?" Charlie asks.

"What-what about me?"

I take a swig of his home-brew.

Charlie's looking at me with those bushy eyebrows raised.

"Oh I don't know Charlie. I can't dream for myself. Just you and Jenny."

He takes back the Mason jar.

"Come on man. I wanna know."

I really don't know. Never thought about it. Never thought about my life after this.

"I guess school maybe. No wedding bells. No kids. Gotta piss my old man off, too, right? Maybe you guys–you and Jenny–maybe you will let me take care of the girls sometimes. I don't know."

It'll never happen.

Charlie hands me the jar. I spill a bit.

"I do know something for sure Charlie. For sure though your gravestone's gonna say Chuck-Chik."

I look over at Charlie. I can't stand to see him sad.

I try to joke: "'Cause gravestones are assholes!"

Charlie snorts.

I'm chugging the mix. I can't help myself.

"Your chunk of granite," I say "... even after... maybe 'cause Jenny's dead or just she can't anymore... I'm gonna look after you Charlie. I'm gonna keep looking after you even when you're gone. I swear it."

And I think, what if? What if we all go on like this? Me watching him watching her, all in a line. Like when we were kids in a massage line in front of *The Days of Our Lives* fighting over the front spot. All I remember from the whole show is the creepy music and the hour glass. I was too busy kneading Charlie's back.

Or what if I got up and left? Would I end up in Paris giving magnificent head under the Eiffel tower in the rain? After the divorce, would Charlie find me in an opium den in India and demand that I put into practice all that he taught me? Would he command, "Get down on your knees and pray before the almighty altar of Charlie!" with a gigantic erection in his pants? Would I gladly repent?

I look at Charlie and he's gone, somewhere else, watching and waiting for Jenny, forever.

I drink hard from the bottle I brought.

And read: Charles Cicarelli, and think Charlie. God! even Chuck-Chik would have been better! I kneel on the wet grass and lean forward. And whisper, "But then, Charlie, all that's left of you is stone," and I stare at nothing but the trees for a long time.

I TEND TO THE TAIL END

The girls I work with over the summer in The Bay's Ladies Accessories Department decide that they want to have a "wild" night. They think it's a good idea to take me out with them.

I know I am headed for trouble. One of these blonde, casual-wear, nubile braindeads is my floor manager. I like her. She's nice, in her context.

When we're at the swank club, I know the bartender. I fucked his roommate and later the same night, him. He sends free drinks our way.

The girls I am with finally catch the attention of some oversized, jock-frat-Bay street boys and, hell, I know I am in for a hard time picking up.

My floor manager swings her long blonde hair over her back revealing her Wonderbra breasts. I introduce myself as Eugene. I can't compete with blonde and breasts without the quirk.

Blondey smiles and flirts. Me—I puke on Jare's shoes and drag him to the door by his tie, screaming, "What? Don't you wanna have a good time?"

Work. Big Boss Blond calls me into the office. *Fuck! Fuck! Fuck!*

"You're cray-zeee!" she squeals, and it hurts my fucking head but at least I still have a job.

She smiles, and asks me how my night with Jare went. I defer.

"How was your night with ah... guy?"

"When we went home, he told me he loved me."

Maybe it's that I'm hung, or maybe it's that she seemed to like me all cray-zeee-like, but, whatever, I decide to tell her the truth.

"Jare bent me over my kitchen sink and asked if he could ass fuck me."

Blondey stares blankly. I'm in for it. I've crossed the goddamn line. I rewrite my resume in my head.

She's staring, earnest, saying nothing, and then...

"I wish someone would say they wanted to ass fuck me."

Jesus Christ! My world is exploding. I have a thought deeper than I've ever had. I have an Epiphany.

Gay men and porno whores have hoarded all ass action. And sure, I may seem biased because I belong to the latter category; I love to suck cock and have a landing strip groomed into my bald eagle snatch, but Blondey's words kick me in the kiester and I see the light: *Everybody loves the ass fucking!*

LESSONS

One: 1992. Scott Yang.

The first time I let a hot rod ride up my homo zone,
I was a born again virgin. I wanted sex, but I didn't
want it to count. Ass fucking seemed like the only
solution for keeping me pure.

I went to the washroom after it was all over. When
I stood up to flush the toilet, I made a crucial mistake.
"Don't look down" is a rule that applies as well to heights
as it does to ass virgins' first trips to the washroom post-fuck.
Before my hand could hit the silver release handle on
the tank, the view in the bowl made me pass-out
and I rapped my head off the porcelain.

Scott Yang was bopping up and down playing guitar
when I finally came-to. Before helping me off the floor,
he put away his guitar and shoved modeling pictures
of himself in my face. He was having
a blast.

I asked him to take me home.

Fuck The Asshole. Do Not Be The Asshole.

Two: 2002. The second time. Richard Riley.

I got around to desiring the sweet meat between my cheeks again in the first year of my MA. What can I say? My mind frame was akin to that of the giggly Porky movies' sorority girls in pink teddies or hot pants and nipple popper tank tops; I was just waiting for the right man to show me the ropes of a new fucktastic experience. Being a near novice to the whole thing, there were physical effects I did not expect.

Richard and I were taking a shower, and I felt like exploring my newly ravished anus. My hole was goddamn huge! I screamed at Rich, "Holy shit, dude! I could shove a Nalgene bottle up my ass."

I panicked. I thought my asshole would never return to its formerly pursed perfection. What did it mean to have a constantly open orifice? Would I be able to hold in my farts? Did I need Depends?

Do not Panic. Things Return to Normal.

Three: 2002. Walter Kerns.

When Walter and I were driving to Halifax, he turned his attention from the road to me. We were sharing one of those road-trip moments of regretful honesty.

He told me that while masturbating he had once taken an English cucumber up the ass. It really got him off. I was baffled that anyone could get that many inches of food *up* his shit shaft.

Later, when Walter bought me a bright pink vibrator, I couldn't resist the urge to make him hurt *so good.* I got him to beat-off while I massaged his insides with my fuchsia cock engine.

Walter bought a John Cougar Mellencamp CD the following morning.

Straight Men Like Things up Their Asses. It Is Fun for Everyone to Put Things up Ass.

◎

Last night, my epileptic lover turned over to spoon me and said, "I think it'd be really cool to fuck me while I was *grand mal*ing. I'd be all tense and jerky and shit. It'd be a fucking ride, baby."

This, from a guy, who, when I'm giving him a blowjob, won't let me stick a finger up his ass.

Eva a SWF 5' 6" Montreal native living and working in Toronto. Eva is a non-smoker who rarely drinks. But make no mistake, she's a spunky, fun and energetic Leo. Eva has her MA in English Literature from Concordia, is an aspiring boxer, and she works out six days a week. Eva enjoys running, yoga, and long bike rides. She adores petting puppy golden retrievers.

Love her!